Scarily Ever Laughter Tale 3

Snow Fright

This book is a work of fiction. Names characters, places, and incidents are either products of the author's imagination or are used fictitiously. Any resemblance to actual events or locales or persons, living or dead, is entirely coincidental and not intended by the author.

Summary: When Sarah White falls through a magic mirror on her twelfth birthday, she must escape the Underworld and a zombie illness in order to rescue her friends from Mr. Death.

BISAC: JUVENILE FICTION/Horror. JUVENILE FICTION/Paranormal, Occult & Supernatural. JUVENILE FICTION/Fairy tales & Folklore/Adaptations

For more information about this title, write us at Mystery Goose Press P.O. Box 86627 Vint Hill, VA 20187

Printed in the United States of America
Library of Congress Control Number:
2019918358

Paperback ISBN: 978-1-948882-14-9
Also available as an ebook

SNOW FRIGHT

Scarily Ever Laughter Tale 3

AMIE BORST
BETHANIE BORST

Illustrated by
ROCH HERCKA

Chapter 1

"**D**on't hate me because I'm beautiful." Gazing at my reflection, I fluffed my hair, the dark curls bouncing in the palm of my hand. My lips parted and a smile spread across my face as I studied the happy expression in the mirror. Honestly, I knew today would be wonderfully perfect the moment I woke up. It was my birthday, after all.

My thoughts were rudely interrupted by an alarm buzzing. I skidded to my bedside, slapping the annoyance into silence. "Wake up, Rose," I said to my half-sister. It was the same thing I'd done and said every day for as long as I could remember.

Rose rolled over and pulled the blankets over her head. "It's too early," she groaned.

"Whatever. Stay in bed until the last minute and crawl out looking like the undead." I tossed a pillow at her head. "See if I care." Clothes flew over my shoulder as I rummaged through my dresser looking for the perfect birthday outfit. Deciding on a pair of jeans, I slipped them on along with my favorite boy band t-shirt.

Still ignoring Rose, I brushed my teeth then ran down-stairs to the kitchen where I found my little brother, Tommy, sitting in his high chair. "Morning Tommy."

Ruffling his hair, I sat next to him watching as he sucked his thumb even though he was almost three years old. He seemed perpetually doomed to the fate of staying small since he hadn't grown much taller than a garden gnome. And staying a baby because my parents pampered him. "Morning Mom, Dad."

"Good morning," Dad mumbled. He hadn't taken his eyes off his newspaper since I walked into the room but acknowledged me with a nod. Sporting his robe, striped pajamas, and brown, loafer-style slippers, it appeared that he had no intention of going to work. He cleared his throat with his fist in front of his mouth.

What? No happy birthday? "Are you feeling alright?" Dad never stayed home so maybe he was coming down with something.

"Huh?" He folded the corner of his paper down so only his eyes peered over the edge. From what I could see, he appeared just fine.

"You're in your pajamas," I said. "You're usually ready for work by now."

"There's an early present for you." Mom interrupted by gesturing toward a small box on the kitchen counter.

I leapt from my seat and swiped the box. "Can I open it?" The gift was tiny, and a jingle sounded when I shook it, but there were no other hints to reveal its contents.

Rose stumbled into the room, eyes still caked with sleep and her hair a disheveled mess. Her archery case was tucked under her arm.

Rose finger-combed her hair out of her eyes before plopping down into a chair on the other side of Tommy.

She pulled the archery tubing from her case and took aim at the cereal box in front of her.

Mom gathered Rose's hair into a ponytail. Rose jerked away. "Stop it."

With a heavy sigh, Mom pulled the elastic from Rose's hair then planted a kiss on my cheek. "Of course, you can. It's your special day. Go on and open it. It's just a little something to start your birthday off right." Mom went to the counter and returned with a plate of food. She tried to coax Tommy into taking his thumb out of his mouth. "It's scrambled eggs."

"Gross!" I held the box at arm's length, plugged my nose and shook my head. "Why would you wrap that?"

"They aren't for you, dummy." Rose's eyes darted toward Tommy, who was busy smearing yellow and red glops of ketchup-covered eggs on his tray. Some of it ended up in his hair.

My cheeks flushed. "Oh."

Rose resumed making pretend shooting motions with her arms, still trying to take down the cereal box in front of her. I rolled my eyes but, unfortunately, she happened to look up at that exact moment. "Don't judge me. I need to practice."

My eyes darted back to the boxed wrapped up with pretty paper and a bow. "Whatever."

"Well, you gonna open it?" Rose released the tubing and it missed, smacking the wall instead with a thwack. She huffed and flicked the box over with her finger.

"Yes." I sighed. Of course I was going to open it. Did I want to do it on her demand? Not exactly. I held the gift in the air like it was a precious jewel for all to observe.

Mom shoveled a spoonful of egg into Tommy's mouth. He laughed and half of it came flying back out, barely missing Mom's eye. "Tom. Would you please just eat?" Her tone and gritted teeth told me her frustration level had just escalated from zero to nine but somehow, she managed to remain calm despite it. Always collected. That was my mother.

Without another moment of hesitation, I tore the ribbon off the mystery package. I peeled back the paper and gently lifted the lid. Nestled between layers of tissue paper was a flower hairclip in my favorite shade of purple. When I lifted it out, I saw what had made the jingling sound; a silver ball no larger than a dime made up the center of the flower. "I love it," I said, remembering my childhood enchantment with fairies. Surely this was my mom's way of asking me not to grow up too fast.

Dad peered over his newspaper, watching the entire scene. He smiled, sipped his water, and started to read his paper again.

I pulled the top of his paper down, forcing him to make eye contract. "Why are you still in your pajamas?"

"Oh." He laughed and placed the paper in his lap. "Thought I'd stay home to help Mom with the party preparations."

"The party!" I squealed. My enthusiasm displayed itself in a fit of small bounces on my chair. "But that isn't until Saturday."

Rose rolled her eyes. "Puh-lease don't do that in public."

"But we're not in public." My brow furrowed.

Rose narrowed her eyes at the back of the cereal box.

"You don't like it when I'm happy?" As if she was any less embarrassing. Rose's infatuation with archery wasn't exactly normal.

"Not when you look like a moron, I don't."

Maybe Rose was right. The last thing I wanted was to look like I didn't fit in. But I made a face at her anyway because I didn't need her telling me what to do.

"That's enough, ladies." Mom wiped Tommy's face. Her attempts to feed him were futile. Though if her intent was to feed the highchair, she scored big time! "I realize the party isn't for two more days, so could we please save the drama for later? I'm feeling a little overwhelmed." She gestured toward Tommy and that was all the explanation I needed. "Now finish getting ready for school."

I glanced down at my new barrette. If I wanted to wear it to school, the jeans and t-shirt would never do. This required a change of clothes. There's no way I'd leave this house letting people believe I couldn't color coordinate. Waving a piece of toast in the air, I hopped up from my chair and proclaimed, "I'm going to change my clothes."

Climbing the stairs two at a time, and devouring the toast just as quickly, I paused when I reached the top. I had an idea!

I snuck into my room and quietly slid open Rose's dresser drawer until I found her most treasured of treasures: her jewelry box. The one her dad had made for her. The dad that left when she was only a baby. The same dad she's never heard from since.

The box lay in the bottom drawer, shimmering and glittering with its inlay of crystals. I pried open the top, and inside I saw the very thing I was after, the necklace from Grandma Millie. Silver scroll work surrounded a small, iridescent opal and hung from a matching silver chain. Wrapping my fingers around it, I slid it into my pocket then tiptoed off to my side of the room.

Pulling a small section of hair back, I clipped in the new barrette and suddenly knew the perfect out fit to go with it. I flew to my closet and grabbed my ruffled turquoise swing top dotted with lavender flowers and my denim mini skirt. Later I'd throw on a pair of shoes, so I slipped on some soft white socks.

Once dressed, I pulled the necklace from the pocket of my jeans which were now sprawled on the floor. After placing the jewelry around my neck, I admired myself in a small mirror situated on my dresser. The necklace matched the rest of my outfit perfectly and Rose certainly wouldn't mind if I borrowed it just this once. Well, actually, she would. That's why I had to sneak. But it was my birthday and Grandma Millie had promised me one before she moved away. Since she wasn't here to give me the twin necklace, I knew she would have liked to see me wear it on my twelfth birthday, just like Rose did.

The necklace had graced my neck for a total of twenty-eight seconds when I heard Rose's stomping. She stormed into our room and opened the very drawer I'd just rifled through. She pulled out her jewelry box, opened it, and then slowly turned toward me, her eyes narrowed.

Frozen. That's what I was. Frozen in fear. Ten. Nine. Eight... I counted to myself. If Rose's behavior was as predictable as worms in a corpse, then she'd be throwing a tantrum by the time I reached five.

Without saying a word, she stomped out, her feet like heavy bricks.

Seven. Six. Five.

Still frozen, I diverted my eyes to the second hand on the clock. Weird. Guess I was wrong about her. Hey, I can't be right one-hundred percent of the time.

Four? Three?

Maybe she wasn't upset that I'd borrowed her necklace. Oh man. What else would make her glare at me though?

"Two." My breath came in a hot, heavy whisper.

"One," Rose said as she barged her way into our room, her bow drawn.

Chapter 2

"**I** told you." Her arms shook with the effort of holding the bow string. Although she stood a good eight feet away, the arrow stared me down, right in the middle of my forehead.

Yikes! My heart thumped rapidly in my chest. She really meant business. "You told me," I gulped.

"I. Told. You," Rose said through gritted teeth. "Don't

take my necklace without my permission. Ever."

"But it matches my outfit, and I wanted to look nice on my birthday and wanted to impress—"

"Impress…? Impress who?"

I shook my head.

"You're such a girly girl. Why do you even care what other people think?"

"What?" I flung a strand of hair over my shoulder. "You mean, you think I should look like you instead?" Her hair was still matted, and in my honest opinion, she looked like the walking dead. How she could go to school looking like that was beyond me. "You're a mess. Just look at you!"

Mom walked into the room. "Excuse me! How many times have I told you not to aim at people?"

"It's foam.," Rose groaned.

"I don't care. Put it away." Mom clicked her way back downstairs.

Rose pursed her lips and released the arrow, a loud snapping sound reverberating off the walls. The arrow soared through the air. It hit the corner of our room and bounced off the wall a gazillion feet from my head. Good thing for me she had terrible aim. And lucky for both of us she was using foam-tipped arrows.

"Whoa, whoa, whoa. Chill out Kat-*miss*."

"Don't call me that. Besides," she drew another arrow, "Coach says I'm improving." She aimed at the ceiling and let the arrow fly. It hit the blades of the fan. The fletching and shaft fell to the ground like shrapnel.

"I see that," I said, stifling a snicker.

"Mark my words."

"Maybe you should try marking your arrows instead."

Steam came out of Rose's red ears like a tea kettle about to burst. Her knuckles turned white from squeezing her hands into fists. As I was about to say something, the doorbell rang. She whipped her head toward the sound, then glared as she turned back. Our eyes locked. I was going to beat her to that door if my life depended on it. After all, it was my birthday. It's not like she would be expecting a delivery.

Truth be told, I wasn't expecting one either.

As if we'd read each other's minds, we both bolted toward the bedroom door. Our shoulders brushed, and for a split second we were jammed in the doorway, shoulder to shoulder. Rose grunted as she pushed through first. I stumbled forward, my hands reaching out for balance and accidentally weaved my fingers into the knitted hem of Rose's shawl. She choked and instinctively grabbed the fabric. With Rose distracted I sprinted toward the front door.

The bell rang again, and I smoothed my hair out of the way. Straightening my clothes, I cleared my throat. Then I turned the handle and swung the door open.

On the porch stood an average-sized man with a shaved head and a partially grown beard. His tan delivery uniform matched his exposed skin. A tall slender box leaned against him for support. "Are you," he glanced at his clipboard, "Sarah White?"

I nodded. "That's me!"

"Sign here." He shoved a clipboard at my stomach and pulled a pen out from behind his ear.

"What is it?" My fingers scribbled my name a little too eagerly.

"How should I know?"

No need to be snarky. "Oh. Well, do you know who it's from?"

The man bent over, reading the label on the box. "Doesn't say."

"That's odd," Mom said, suddenly peering over my shoulder. Tommy clung to the hem of her long skirt, sucking his thumb. "Maybe it's from your uncle. The one out in Texas."

"I have an uncle in Texas?"

"You know the one. He used to visit when you were small."

My mom. She likes to think I can remember all that stuff that happened when I was three. I could barely feed myself and was probably still in training pants, but yeah, I was going to remember an uncle I'd seen twice that year. Not. "Oh right. *That* uncle," I said sarcastically.

"The one with the beard. He's like a big grizzly bear."

I stared at her.

"My brother, Phillip." She huffed. "Anyway, he was always so good to you. You're one of his favorite nieces you know." She paused a second. "You and your sister, Rose, of course."

"Favorite? Why hasn't he sent a gift any other year?"

Mom blushed and fanned her face. "Twelve is a big one in our family."

I should have made that connection, what with Grandma Millie's necklace and all. Absentmindedly, I touched my neck.

"Package is heavy," the delivery man said, interrupting my mom's road trip down memory lane.

Rose stood in the corner, arms crossed, pouting. "Sarah took my necklace without asking. The one from Grandma Millie."

"Not now, Rose." Mom rubbed her forehead. "Can't you see we're busy here?"

The delivery man tapped the top of the box. "Think you can handle it?"

"We've got it under control." I reached for the corner.

"Great. Have a nice day." He leaned the package toward me, and it fell against my shoulder with a thud.

"Umpf. You too," I said with a pained grunt.

Mom picked up Tommy, who was feverishly rubbing his eyes with the back of his chubby fist. She used the hem of her shirt to wipe his snotty nose. *Gross.*

"I think somebody's tired." Mom kissed his forehead. "Time for a nap."

"Little. Help. Here," I panted.

"Oh. Oh!" Mom handed Tommy off to Rose. "Please put your brother down for a nap."

"At this hour?" Rose questioned. Then she mumbled under her breath. "You know he's not really a baby anymore, don't you?" She was really pushing buttons and if she continued, she was going to find the detonator.

Mom snapped her head toward Rose. "He's been up since five. I'd say it's time." I'm guessing she wasn't going to address the other half of Rose's complaint.

Mom secured a corner of the box, lifting it off my shoulder. "Shall we take it inside?"

"We shall." What? Who was I and why did such strange words come from my mouth? "I mean, yeah. Let's take it in."

As I stumbled over the threshold, I noticed the familiar shaggy hair of Hunter, who stood across the street. "Hunter?" I called. When our eyes met, he ducked behind a tree.

Chapter 3

"Think we might need another set of hands." Mom's face screwed up as she lifted one end with a grunt. "Roooose! Come help us!"

"She's putting Tommy down, remember?" Did she really forget that quickly? And why couldn't Dad help?

Before Mom could acknowledge me, Rose entered the room, leaned against a wall and folded her arms indignantly. Instead of pouting, she smirked.

"Give us a hand." Mom blew a puff of air from her pursed lips, sending her bangs for a ride.

"Oh no. You're not roping me into this one." Rose inched away, one step at a time.

"Fine. Be that way. See if I'll help you when you have a package delivered on *your* birthday." *Ha. Like anyone would send her anything.*

"I did my job. I put Tommy down for his mid-morning snooze." Rose stared at my throat. "Plus, you're still wearing my necklace."

"Get over it and let your sister wear it. Grandma Millie would have wanted it that way."

"But—but…That's not fair! It's mine!" Rose stomped her foot.

For some reason this made my mom snap. "Rose Red."

Her lips pursed so tight and her eyes narrowed so slim, she looked like a squinting duck. But really, I knew she was expressing something between disappointment and anger. "That's enough out of you."

Rose huffed dramatically as she hoisted the front end of the box. "Fine. Wear the necklace. See if I care."

Mom squared her shoulders as she lifted the box, and the three of us carried it into the living room. "Where do you want it?"

I hadn't thought about that part. I mean, who knew what was in it? Maybe I wouldn't even want what was inside. But if it was something totally awesome, it needed to be out of Tommy's reach. That little mole rat put his grubby hands on everything. "My room," I blurted before I could think it through any further.

"All the way up the stairs?" Rose whined because, well, because she could.

"How about we just set it here for now?" A bead of sweat dripped off of Mom's nose.

We placed the box against the wall in the living room near the bottom of the staircase. Rose groaned and marched up the stairs, leaving Mom and I to stare at the package.

"Let me get you a pair of scissors." Mom wiped more sweat from her brow, nodded, and walked off. She returned a moment later.

"Thanks," I said, taking the scissors and running the blade along the seam of the box. The tape was stickier than I expected. I tugged. I pulled. I twisted. I jabbed. None of my super-scientific, awesome, well-thought-out methods worked. As a last resort, I lunged the tip of the scissors into the tape and tugged backward with all my strength. The tape gave a little. Hopeful, I adjusted my position and made one final tug. The scissors gave way and I toppled backward, head over heels.

Dad suddenly walked into the room. "You're never going to open the package like that." He held out his hand and I placed the scissors in his open palm. With one swift motion he zipped through the tape and opened the package.

"I loosened it for you," I said, defensively.

Dad smirked. "So, what'd you get?"

I pulled myself up and peered into the box. *Packing peanuts. Lots of them.* I moved them out of the way and exposed a shiny reflective surface. "A mirror!"

"Really?" Dad tore away at the rest of the cardboard, revealing the gift; a full-length mirror with a gorgeous wood frame.

The frame had been intricately carved with the tiniest details. A forest of trees with long, leafless branches arched across the top of the mirror, intertwining into knotted vines. Small bulbous-type flowers lined up in rows along the bottom. Birds sat motionless within the branches of the trees.

"Whoa," I said, breathing the word instead of speaking it. "Who sent this?" One thing I knew for sure, whoever it was knew me well. A mirror was a perfect gift and the detail made me feel special. Whoever made it put a lot of time into it. I smiled at the reflection staring back at me.

"That can't possibly be from your uncle. I mean, unless he's taken up woodworking." Mom peeled the label off the box and removed the shipping information from the plastic cover. She unfolded the paper and turned it over in her hands. "It doesn't say." She bustled over to inspect the mirror. "Sure is pretty though."

"A real beauty," Dad added, giving a long, low whistle. "That's craftsmanship right there. Haven't seen something of that quality in a long time. At least not since I was a boy when my mother——"

"Can I put it in my room now?" I asked, cutting him off. No time for Dad's long-winded stories.

"Will you help her carry it up the stairs?" Mom turned to Dad. That was mom talk for, *You're going to do this—like it or not—because it's my girl's special day. And because I lugged it inside and am too tired to carry that sucker all the way up the stairs.*

"Sure, sure," Dad said, knowing that look all too well.

"Okay, meet you there." I raced up the steps two by two and burst into our room. "Rose! Rose! You'll never believe it—I got a mirror!"

Rose startled and released the bowstring, which attacked her arm. She winced, dropped the bow and immediately nursed the large red welt that festered on the inside of her forearm. "What do you want? An award?"

"Oh sorry."

She scowled at me. "No, I'm fine. It's not like my arm is burning from the pain of a string with a sixteen-pound draw weight slapping against it." Rose blew a strand of hair from her face and turned away. She pulled back again and just as she came to a full draw, Dad hollered.

"Rose, I could use a hand with this thing." Dad's voice carried up the stairs so loud it was like he was standing right outside our door.

Rose's hand slipped and the bowstring released. It slapped her arm again, directly adjacent to the first welt. Her good hand shot into the air and she muffled her scream into the crook of her elbow. Tears welled up in her eyes. My jaw went slack feeling almost as stunned as she was. *That had to hurt.* A second angry red mark burst its ugly head on her fair skin.

"I'm going downstairs now," Rose said. At least that's what I think she said, because she marched out of the room and stomped down the stairs. But honestly, I could hardly understand her, as it sounded more like, "Imhoinnownfairshow."

I skipped down the stairs after her only to see Dad using the mirror to hold himself up. "Let's get this sucker up there, shall we?" Dad gestured, wobbling the mirror in place. "All hands-on deck."

"You mean I really have to help?" Rose held out her bruised arm.

Mom walked up behind her and rubbed the angry mark. "I'll get you some ice as soon as we're done." She hugged Rose's shoulders. "You really should be careful with that bow. You'll shoot your eye out."

"Or give yourself a winner." Dad wagged a finger at Rose's bruise. The four of us carried the mirror up the stairs to my room. "Alright then," he said, taking a sweeping inventory of free space. "So, where did you want it?"

"Over there." I motioned by tipping my head toward the corner. "Put it between the window and my dresser."

"Fine, we'll do it," Rose huffed. "But I'm not helping you with anything else today."

We lowered it into position and Mom panted. "Be nice, Rose." She smiled through beads of sweat on her upper lip.

"Okay then." Dad leaned the mirror against the wall.

"Thanks." My eyes stayed glued on it; I was in awe of the beauty before me. My beauty, that is.

"Happy birthday." Dad ruffled my hair as he left the room.

"Looks like it was made just for you. Enjoy it." Mom smiled warmly.

"Can I?" Rose started toward the mirror, suddenly fascinated.

But I refused to step out of the way, planting my feet firmly in place. Fluffing my hair, I admired myself. I reached for a compact and swept blush on my cheeks and smiled.

"Gosh, Sarah," Rose said, suddenly standing behind me. "You're as shallow as a kiddy pool."

"Shut up!" I shouted. "Just—just get out of here." I shooed Rose out of the room. She resisted, but I won. As soon as she was in the hall, I slammed the door and turned the lock.

"Let me in you little twerp," Rose said.

"Not on your life," I said as I collapsed against the door.

"Fine. Have it your way." Rose huffed. Her footfalls soon echoed softly down the stairs.

With a heavy sigh, I tipped my head back. As I did, something caught my eye in the reflection of the mirror. I blinked. Nah, I was seeing things. But then, I wasn't. Because a shadow darted across the mirror. I shook my head. It was gone. Maybe not.

I inched my way toward it. As I got closer, more movement outside the window demanded my attention. When I glanced out, I realized that's all it was. The sun casting shadows in the yard. As I carefully surveyed the property, searching for what would make such a strange shadow on my mirror, I saw Hunter. As soon as our eyes met, he ducked behind a tree. Again.

Chapter 4

"Hunter!" I banged on the glass with the palm of my hands. "Hunter! Hunter!" His gaze remained fixed elsewhere, his focus fully attending to something not within my line of sight. "Hunter?" I tapped the glass one more time. Still, he didn't move. Maybe if I opened the window, he'd be able to hear me. Except, I quickly realized that Dad had painted it shut last summer. Claimed it needed a fresh coat because it hadn't been done in ages. Normally, I was happy to indulge Dad in his constant projects around the house...until now when I really needed that window open.

The paint had fixed the window shut but I banged along the edge until the seal popped. The window jerked open, inch by inch. Leaning out over the sill, I waved at Hunter. "What are you doing?"

Hunter's head jerked up until his gaze caught mine. His eyes widened, and then he dashed off.

"Wait." My hand shot out again to wave, but I lost my balance and slipped, falling halfway out the window. My heart beat rapidly, like a rabbit on too much caffeinated soda. My body trembled as I inched my way back inside, closing the window with an uncertain but irritated *humpf*. "That was a close one."

Swirling around, I caught movement in the mirror again. I glanced outside but there weren't any shadows. Placing my palm against the shiny reflection I worried that something felt off, but I couldn't figure out what. The mirror suddenly rippled. "What on earth…?" My skin crawled. "What was that?" POP! Something pinged inside my brain. I rubbed my head.

BRAIN FREEZE

Why hello, beautiful! I'm talking to you. Yes, you. Call me Steve.

"What?" I searched the room for the voice. "Who's there?" When no response came, I figured I was just hearing things. Ignoring it, I turned back to my reflection and fluttered my eyelashes. "Mirror, mirror, on the wall. Who's the fairest of them all?" I joked. A blue glow from my necklace radiated color as it pulsed. "That's odd." I stepped closer, touching my fingertips to the mirror's surface, but the light disappeared. Insecurity suddenly grabbed my throat. My image seemed to ripple in the mirror and then POP! I felt another ping in my brain. "What the …what?"

BRAIN FREEZE

Heehee. I'm Slimy. Verrrrry slimy. Just like your brain. Nice to meet you, Sarah!

Another, different voice, oozing in my head just like, well, slime. Whirling around, my head spun. What was happening? "Who is that? Hunter? Are you playing a joke on me?" I shook my head trying to get the voices to go away and noticed the fluorescent light of my bedside lamp glowing behind me. My skin crawled. "Creepy! I thought I turned that off."

POP! Another sharp pain struck inside my head.

BRAIN FREEZE

Yesssss, you rang? My name is Creeeeeepy and you should be creeped out. We're heeeerrrreeee!

"You better knock that off!" I yelled. "This isn't funny!" I closed my eyes. Birthday excitement was messing with my head. That was all. I wasn't hearing voices. That would never happen to me. If it did, I certainly couldn't tell anyone. Especially my friends. Friends who would be coming to my birthday party. *Yes, that's it. Think good, happy thoughts.* I opened my eyes with a bright smile, and blanched as I saw another ripple form on the glass.

PING! POP! POP! PING! The worst headache I'd ever had struck me, followed by four brand new voices.

BRAIN FREEZE

Stinky is at your command. *burps* I know some other things that are stinky. Have you smelled my farts lately? What have I been eating anyway?

Icky here. *sneezes* Oh yeah? Well, try having a constant cold.

Yucky's the name, disgusting's my game. By the way, you've got a pimple on your chin. Mind sharing? They're full of protein.

My name is Crawly. Heh-heh. If you like creepy, crawly things, maybe some spiders will join us. But if not, then I can fulfill the role.

"Whoa. What was that all about?" I stumbled backward, falling to the floor. "I don't know who is doing this but it's not funny. Get out of here! Stop teasing me!" My head pounded and I rubbed it with my palm. Okay, maybe addressing the weird voices in my head wasn't the way to prove I hadn't lost my mind, but I couldn't help it.

The mirror suddenly lit up like fireworks on the fourth of July. I scrambled to my feet and stepped closer. A bolt of blue light, just like lightning flashed in the mirror. "What's that?" I whispered as I shook my head. "First voices then this?"

BRAIN FREEZE

Steve: Well, it looks like we're all here! Meet Stinky.

Stinky: Yo! Pardon the noise. And the smell. *burps* Wait a minute. I already introduced myself.
Steve: Sorry.
Stinky: No problem. Carry on.
Creepy: I'll get you!
Steve: Good. I've got it from here guys. Ignore him. Creepy is all talk.
Creepy: That's meeeee. Allllll tallllllk. Wait a minute!
Steve: Looks like this is going to be more difficult than I thought. There's seven of us. Stinky, Crawly, Icky, Yucky, Slimy, Creepy. And finally, there's me. I'm Steve. *waves*

I straightened my shoulders and looked at my reflection head on. "Well, Stinky, Crawly, Icky, Yucky, Slimy, Creepy and . . . and Steve, you can go find some other brain to fester in, because I am not hearing voices and I am hereby pretending you don't exist. So there."

BRAIN FREEZE

Icky: Okay, but that zit definitely exists.
Slimy: That's right. You're ugly.
Stinky: And gross. *scratches hairy chest* Just like me. We're two peas in a pod.
Steve: Poor girl. She's going to have it rough.

I rubbed my head. If my brain was playing a trick on me, why was it being so mean? I'd never think such awful things like that. I bit my lip, my chest aching. Leaning in closer to the mirror, I saw the pimple they were talking about. Those voices were right. How could anyone ever like me with such a disgusting zit on my face?

BRAIN FREEZE

Crawly: You'll never fit in.
Creepy: You'll neveeeeer be preeeeeetty enough.

Turning away from the mirror, I blinked away the tears and sat on the floor. Why would I think such horrible things about myself? I mean, sure I felt insecure at times, especially when I really wanted people to like me, but I'd never let anyone know that.

When I turned back, the reflection in the mirror was different. Not only did it not quite look like me but the girl in the mirror was standing while I was still sitting on the floor. My jaw came unhinged. "How is that possible?" The girl in the mirror fiddled with the pendant on Grandma Millie's necklace and it began to glow. I glanced down at the necklace on my own neck in disbelief. "No way," I whispered, my mouth feeling unusually dry, like I'd been to the dentist and had cotton balls stuffed there. "That's…"

Steve: Impossible.

"Impossible." My heart leapt in my chest. What the… what? My hands were cold and clammy as I wrung them together. "I've lost my mind." The words squeaked out, refusing to admit they were true.

Creepy: Yaaaaassss you haaaaave. It's delicious, too.

"No. I'm just tired." But I couldn't really be sure about that. The reflection in the mirror appeared to have a mind of its own. Plus, it really did seem as if there were voices carrying on a conversation inside my brain. Voices that introduced themselves. Voices not only with names but also individual personalities. If I was just talking to myself, I'd chosen a really strange way to do it.

BRAIN FREEZE

Icky: Sick *achoo!* and tired.

"Go away!" I shouted at the voices. "I'm not sick. I'm excited about my birthday." I nodded. "I'm overly excited. And I'm having hallucinations!" That's it! Dehydration causes hallucinations. I licked my lips remembering the cotton ball dryness a moment ago. I was dehydrated. That was all. A drink. That's exactly what I needed. I dashed into the bathroom and returned with a glass of water, gulped it down, and wiped my mouth.

"I was just thirsty," I said aloud. This time, my reflection was completely the same as my own, the girl's mouth moving along with mine. Phew! The voices even seemed to quiet down, too.

What a relief! That's all it was. A dehydration hallucination. What a strange way to start my birthday. Lifting my hand, I crept my fingers closer to the mirror, the icy glass so cold I could feel it even inches away.

The doorbell rang and my heart nearly exploded out of my chest. "I'll get it!" I ran down the stairs, straight to the entryway but slipped on the hardwood floor and slammed into the door.

"Chickadee!" Cindy, my BFF, squealed. A breeze blew her blonde hair into her face and it stuck to her lip gloss.

"Chickeroo!" I threw myself out the door, ignoring her attempt to de-gloss the spot on her hair. My arms nearly strangled her in a huge hug. Hopefully she wouldn't notice how jittery I was. Or that I was losing my mind.

"Happy birthday!" she said handing me a small, wrapped gift. "Just a little something to hold you over until the party this weekend."

"Oh! That's so sweet of you. Thanks." My hand trembled a little bit, and I gripped the gift tighter.

Cindy did a little excited hop from foot to foot.

"What's wrong?"

"Open it!" she said.

Forcing my hands not to tremble, I slowly unwrapped the gift. There was a porcelain box beneath the wrapping. The lid slid off easily and inside there was half of a friendship bracelet. But it wasn't just any friendship bracelet; it had a headstone charm on it. And there was a creepy bird and a daisy. I furrowed my brow. What an odd gift.

Cindy must have read the expression on my face and recovered quickly. "Why don't I put it on for you?" She grabbed my hand before I could object and clasped the bracelet on my wrist. "We're a match." Cindy held up her arm revealing a piece of jewelry. She put her wrist next to mine and the halves clicked together. "See? It says, 'Best Friends Forever.'"

"Oh wow. Thanks. I love it!" Even if the headstone charm was a bit weird.

Cindy beamed. "I knew you would."

"Who's here?" Mom called from the kitchen.

"It's Cindy," I hollered back just as Rose came running into the room.

"Hey." Rose nodded at Cindy in acknowledgement. Why she treated Cindy decent but not me is something I would never understand. "We better hurry," Rose said, pointing to the clock. "We'll miss the bus." She threw her backpack over her shoulder and tossed mine at my feet.

I slipped my arms through the strap as a funny feeling climbed up my throat, like a spider weaving its web. "There's Hunter!" I said, pointing into the street. I tried to sound enthusiastic despite the strange sensation that felt vaguely like a warning.

Chapter 5

When Cindy and I reached our lockers, the urge to tell her about the mirror itched me something fierce. Even though I wasn't sure what to say, a nagging feeling warned me that she should know. On the other hand, if I told her about the strange things that had happened – the reflection and eerie voices – she may think I'd lost my ever-loving mind.

My brain was playing tricks and it scared me. A lot. But I needed to tell someone. "The weirdest—"

"Oh, hey! Did I mention that I have another present for you?" Cindy interrupted, silencing my moment of bravery.

"Really?" I brightened.

"I wanted to bring it to your house this morning but Momster—" She paused, then giggled. Cindy had made quite the adjustment with her stepmom, but sometimes she slipped. I guess I couldn't blame her. I think I'd have a hard time, too. "I mean, Tabitha said I should bring it by your house on Saturday so you could open it at the party."

"Mort and Drac said I should bring my gift then, too." Scarlet appeared, as if from thin air, nearly giving me a heart attack. "But only after I have a snack."

Cindy and Scarlet exchanged looks and laughed, and I felt like I was missing out on a joke.

"Thanks guys," I said, draping my arms over their shoulders, a sense of calm washing over me just being surrounded by my friends. There was no need to mention the mirror (or the voices) after all. The whole thing was just silly.

Footsteps approached from behind and a pair of hands suddenly grabbed me around the waist. "Hunter," I said, nearly jumping out of my skin. Laughing, I tried to hide how jittery I felt. "You scared me." He'd been acting so weird before school, creeping around outside my window.

"Happy birthday," he said, holding out a bouquet of daisies. The roots were still attached, and a clump of dirt dangled from them.

"Thanks," I said with a smile.

"Happy birthday," Ethan shouted from halfway down the hall. He waved than ran toward us, stopping between Scarlet and Cindy.

"Nice job, wolfboy." Scarlet said staring at the daises Hunter had given me. She grimaced as Ethan elbowed her in the ribs. "I mean, er, Mr. Peterkin will go postal when he sees you took those straight from his perfectly manicured garden."

Hunter's face grew red with embarrassment. Ohhhhh, that's why he had been hanging around. I should have figured that my major crush wasn't really a stalker.

"I'm sure he'll never notice," Cindy chimed in. But I could tell by the way she gulped after she said it, that she was lying through her perfectly white teeth.

It didn't take a genius to know that Mr. Peterkin was a fanatic about his yard. Everyone knows that dogs and bikes don't return if they're left within a ten-foot radius of his property. Rumor had it, though, that he nearly died recently when he thought he saw a skeleton outside his window. Guess even he has his limits.

"I'll make him a pie," Hunter said, reaching for my backpack.

"Better make it pumpkin," Cindy said with a wink.

Everyone laughed knowing Mr. Peterkin's affinity with the giant squash.

While they carried on, talking and chatting away, I placed the flowers in the top of my locker, the dirt raining down on my head.

"Sound okay to you?" I only heard the tail end of what Hunter said.

"Huh? What?"

"Tell me you missed that entire conversation," he said with a sigh.

Straight faced I said, "I missed that entire conversation."

Scarlet covered her mouth and laughed.

"We were saying that we'd like to come early and help your mom set up for the party," Cindy said, catching me up with their plans.

I shrugged. "I guess."

"Well, your parents won't mind," Scarlet said matter-of-factly. "They seem pretty cool to me."

"Yeah, yeah," I said with a nod. "They're cool, I guess. Maybe my mom will make some snacks to munch on while you work."

"Knowing your mom," Cindy said, "She will probably have an entire feast planned. One big enough to feed an army."

"Yummmm." Scarlet rubbed her belly and smacked her lips. "I hope they'll be some staff sergeants there." She wiped away a wad of drool. "Maybe even Colonial Corn."

"Excuse me?" I said, confused.

"What Scarlet means is she hopes there will be some KETTLE CORN," Hunter shouted that last part as he scratched behind his ear. "Yup. Kettle corn."

"Perfect combination of salty and sweet," Cindy said a bit awkwardly.

There was a brief moment of silence before everyone erupted with laughter. Then the bell rang, and we scattered as quickly as roaches in daylight. "So I'll see you then?" I called to Hunter as he dashed down the hall.

He shot his hand in the air and waved. "Yup," he called back.

My face flushed a very healthy color of pink in excited anticipation.

"Wait up," I called after Cindy and Scarlet. But they were swallowed up by the doorway to their class. "Or... er...I'll just see you later I guess."

The day passed surprisingly fast and as soon as the bell rang, I dumped the contents of my locker into my backpack and zipped it up. Nearly forgetting the daisies Hunter gave me, I opened my locker again. The wilted flowers were in sad shape, but I clasped them tight in my hand anyway. Water would revive them once I was home.

"About Saturday afternoon." Scarlet slammed my locker.

Startled, I jumped back. Sometimes the way she snuck up on people gave me the creeps.

Scarlet looked down and nervously kicked the heel of her foot against the toes on the other. "Is your mom really going to have an army there?" She kicked her toes again. "Because if she is..." her voice trailed off.

My eyebrows knitted together. "What do you mean?"

Baffled, she looked up, her eyes cold. "Cindy said there would be enough food to feed an army." She had a strange tone in her voice. Even seemed a little edgy if you asked me.

"Oh." I chuckled nervously. "That's just a figure of speech."

Scarlet's eyes pierced straight through me. But something else was there. Relief, maybe? "That's good," she said with a sigh. "That's very good."

"You've got problems with soldiers? Or is it just authority in general?"

Scarlet's eyes narrowed. "Something like that."

"Oh." Well, that was as clear as mud. "So, I'll see you at school tomorrow?"

She nodded empathically.

"You don't have to come if you don't want to, you know. To the party, I mean."

It was like Scarlet suddenly snapped out of it because her eyes brightened, and she smiled. "I wouldn't miss it."

"Great." We stood with eyes locked before she finally turned and crept off, her steps as light as air.

That was weird. I shrugged and started in the opposite direction as I pulled my iPod from my bad. That awkward conversation had cost me some time. And the bus. Slipping an ear bud on, I picked up the pace and headed home. I hadn't had a chance to turn on my music when I heard someone calling my name.

"Hold on." Hunter's footsteps were heavy on the pavement as he ran to catch up to me. He bent over, gripping his side as he caught his breath. "You're fast when you wanna be," he said between pants.

"What's up?" I lifted the daises he gave me to my nose, batting my eyelashes.

"I just," he paused, "wanted to make sure that—"

"Let's go Chickeroo!" Cindy charged at me, clasped her hand in mine, and took off running again, dragging me with her.

"I'll see you later!" I waved to Hunter.

"Be careful with reflections," he shouted after me.

Chapter 6

A chill crept over my skin. Reflections? Did he know about my mirror?

Maybe he really was spying on me this morning. My throat felt like I'd tried to swallow too many crackers without any water to wash them down.

"See you soon," Cindy broke free from my grasp as we approached our street.

"Later." My head felt foggy. Like smoke clouded my thoughts. Hunter's comment made me feel leary.

Once Cindy was out of sight, I pushed through the front door, closed it behind me, and then shuffled to the kitchen. While I wasn't thrilled about the idea of home-work on my birthday, I claimed the counter space as my dominion.

"What Sarah doing?" said Tommy's small voice. He didn't speak much more than a few words to anyone except me. In fact, Mom and Dad babied him because of it.

"Grown up stuff." I flipped open my math textbook dreading the hours of algebraic equations. "It's called homework," I said, stabbing my pencil into the binder hole of the notebook.

He pulled his thumb from his mouth and climbed into my lap. "Tommy help?"

"I don't think so little buddy."

Tommy's lips puckered and his shoulders wobbled up and down.

"Don't cry." I snuggled him in my arms. "If you let me finish this, I promise we can play trains later."

Tommy seemed satisfied because he hopped down off my lap and tottered off in that strange way small children do. "I talk to mirror now."

My heart stopped and the hairs on my arms stood on end. I couldn't swallow. Couldn't breathe. "You've been talking to my mirror?" Maybe the voices weren't just in my head after all. "Tommy," I called. "Tom!"

Mom walked into the kitchen. "What's the matter, Sarah?"

"Nothing," Goosebumps popped up all over my arms. "It's..." Maybe I'd just misunderstood Tommy. "It's nothing."

"Well, alright." She fished around in the cupboard not really listening to me.

I finished my last math equation and brought my bag upstairs. Rose lay on her bed reading. From the way she was positioned, I could just make out the title. *Zombie Apocalypse.*

"Don't bug me," she said without moving, her nose still in the book. "I'm reading."

"I wasn't planning on it."

Rose lowered the book and glowered. "Is there something you don't understand about what I just said?"

What was eating her?

"Okay, everybody. Pizza's here!" Dad called.

Rose and I pushed out of the bedroom, shoulder to shoulder, just like we had this morning. As we fought our way down the stairs, Dad kicked the door shut behind him while balancing a bag of groceries in one hand, the boxes of pizza in another.

"Dada!" Tommy toddled over with his arms outstretched.

I grabbed Tommy, lifted him onto my shoulders. We made airplane noises as I flew him around the room. Zooming into the kitchen, Tommy safely landed in the highchair.

"What kind did you get?" Rose asked as Dad placed the pies on the counter.

"Cheese and pepperoni with mushrooms." Dad opened the boxes, revealing the piping-hot pizzas. "Your favorite," he said to Rose with a wink.

"Yes!" Rose's fist pumped.

"Gross. Mushrooms make me feel like I'm eating brains." Why didn't he remember that I hated mushrooms? On my birthday even. I picked the little fungus off one by one, my nose wrinkling in disgust.

"Ewwww." Rose curled her lip. "How would you even know what it's like to eat a brain?"

"Why do you ask such stupid questions?" I threw a mushroom at her. Didn't she understand that it was just something people said? Like a comparison. I bet she had her own that weren't any better.

When we finished eating dinner, Mom placed my favorite brownies on the table. I wasn't a fan of cake, so at least someone remembered something I liked. They sang

"Happy Birthday" before I blew out the candles. Mom and Dad said they were waiting until my party to give me the rest of my presents, which was cool. It just extended the celebration.

When it was bedtime, Rose curled up under the blankets and read from that same stupid zombie book. Her eyes drooped and I knew that it was a matter of time before she'd be fast asleep.

Arms folded behind my head I lay there thinking about my birthday. A soft thud broke my concentration and sent shivers down my spine. Jolting upright, eyes wide, I stared at the mirror. Could it...?

Creepy: Yessss. It could....

The voices were back!

Nah. Impossible. I turned toward Rose, but her eyes were shut tight and her book was on the floor. That must have been the noise I'd heard—the sound of her book dropping.

"That's all it was," I whispered in relief. I tiptoed across the room to pick up the book and turn off her lamp. Yawning, I returned to my bed to do the same. After I snuggled back in, the voices started.

Steve: It wasn't the book.

Throwing the blankets off, I sat up in a start. "Who's there?" Rose snored in response.

Steve: It's us!
Crawly: You haven't forgotten about us, have you?

My eyes darted around the room, my ears on super high alert. "I'm hearing things." Somehow confessing it aloud made me feel more confident that what I'd uttered was true.

Creepy: Of course, you're hearing thingssssss. You're hearing ussssss.
Slimy: Don't ignore us.
Steve: We just want to help...

Chills crept up my arms. *Enough of that,* I warned myself. *You're tired and creeping yourself out.*

I nestled into bed, sleep heavy on my eyes. All I wanted was an uninterrupted slumber to dream about my birthday, my party, and presents. Minutes passed before the strange voices started again.

Stinky: Don't sleep. *farts*
Icky: We need you.

"Why do you need me? What do you want?" My voice wavered. Maybe I really was going crazy.

Breath frozen in my chest the silence proved the voices never existed. Instead a creepy tune began playing. It chimed like an old wind-up jewelry box. The one with the spinning ballerina that I had donated when I turned eight. The tune twanged so loud I couldn't believe that Rose was able to sleep through it.

When the tune wouldn't stop, I sat up. A bright flash lit the room. The surface of the mirror rippled like water. Heinous laughter caused the hairs on my arms to stand. My hands flew up and covered my ears to block out the noise.

The mirror.

The beautiful, ebony-framed mirror was haunted.

Chapter 7

The alarm sounded with a strange crow. I woke suddenly and noticed the time. I leapt out of bed and slid my feet into the slippers neatly tucked under my nightstand. "Get up, Rose," I said with urgency. I'd never overslept. Mostly because I needed sufficient time to beautify myself. "We're late!"

It was unusual, however, that Rose hadn't groaned from her bed about it being too early. It was also unusual that she hadn't then pulled the covers over her head and told me to go away.

As I stood there thinking about the unusual circumstances of the morning, I realized I'd also had strange dreams. The strangest dreams imaginable. Something about a carnival...and a Ferris wheel...horrible laughter, and music.

My heart pounded in my chest.

The mirror.

I didn't dare look at it. Without my permission, my head turned in its direction, eyes narrowing in on its glossy surface.

Nothing. No flash of light. No ripples.

And best of all, no voices.

In disbelief, I tiptoed across the room to the corner

where the mirror stood. My fingers reached out to touch it. They brushed the cool glass. I waited for a spark. A laugh. Something. Anything to tell me I hadn't lost my mind.

Still nothing.

I rubbed the heels of my hand against my eyes. "It was just my imagination. A bad dream. That's all. Nothing else." Then I caught a glimpse of the reflection of the clock behind me and remembered the time. "Oh no!" We were so late.

"Wake up," I called again a little more hastily, my eyes still heavy with sleep. But when I went to her bedside, it was empty! "Oh no. Something's not right about this. Something is very, very wrong." I rushed into the bathroom and nearly stumbled backward when I saw Rose already dressed. She picked up a brush from the edge of the sink and ran it through her curly, red hair. They stretched out into a straight line then sprang back into perfect ringlets. If I had tried that, my hair would have been nothing but frizz.

"What do you want?" She slammed the brush onto the counter.

Why couldn't she just be nice? "Are you ready to go?"

"Obviously I'm more ready than you." She pointed at my pajama top, and although I hadn't paid much attention to my reflection yet, I could only assume she'd also referenced my perfectly coiffed bedhead. A tangled style that usually only afflicted Rose. Not me.

Rose pushed past me, her shoulder slamming into my own. I didn't give her the satisfaction of wincing. The bedroom door slammed shut behind her as she stormed out.

Tiptoeing over to my birthday mirror, I gazed into it while tucking a strand of hair behind my ear. "Don't hate me because I'm beautiful."

Steve: Yes. You are beautiful, Sarah.

"Thank you." A smile tugged at the corner of my mouth. Maybe I wasn't a super model, but I definitely wasn't sitting at the loser table either. But then I gasped realizing the voices were still there. "Guess it wasn't a dream after all." My phone buzzed on the nightstand and I dashed to answer the text. I never, ever received texts so early in the morning. What a strange day this was turning out to be.

Cindy: Don't make plans this weekend

I quickly texted back.

Me: K. But y?

I waited for a response, but none came, so I threw on some clothes that were laying on the floor and bolted to the kitchen for breakfast.

Dad was burning frozen waffles and Mom had curlers

hanging from the ends of her hair. She sat reading the morning paper. Now that was a role reversal. Dad usually wore the curlers.

Tom sat in his high chair neatly eating from a bowl of cereal.

Rose sat prim and proper with a napkin spread across her lap, sipping from a teacup with her pinky in the air.

What a strange situation.

"Everything okay." Dad handed me a plate of blackened discs.

Uhhhh....nope. "Uh-huh." I nodded.

"Great." He handed me a fork. "Eat up."

The doorbell rang just as I'd lifted a bite of burnt waffle to my mouth. My fork clattered as I darted off to answer the door.

Scarlet stood there with Cindy, nearly busting at the seams with excitement as she held out four small slips of paper. "Mort got us tickets to The Hungry Games!" It was the most emotion I'd ever seen from her.

"I've been dying to see that!" I said, hopping from one foot to the other. Rose entered the room and I stopped. She hated when I acted excited. Rose smiled as she neatly slid the backpack onto her shoulders. A snide remark was coming. I just knew it.

"So, do you wanna come?" Scarlet asked me.

"You're going, aren't you?" Cindy nudged my side.

"Are you kidding?" My eyes darted from Rose to my friends. "Of course, I'm in!"

Rose snaked an arm out reaching for the tickets. "You're seeing The Hungry Games?" Her excitement almost hid the hurt that crept onto her face.

"Ummmm yeah." I pushed her back. "Why?"

"Nothing." Rose slowly inched away.

"You can see it with us," Cindy offered.

Rose lit up like the night sky on the Fourth of July. "Really?"

"Sure." Cindy brushed a strand of hair behind her ear. "There's six tickets." She turned to Scarlet. "Mort wouldn't mind, would she?"

"I'm guessing that's why she bought so many in the first place. So you all could come." Scarlet turned and put the tickets in the pocket of her backpack. "Everyone including Winnie and Bertha. And you, too, Rose." Scarlet shrugged, completely unemotional about the whole thing. "And just in case you wanted to know, we missed the bus." She thumbed over her shoulder where the bus roared into gear, heading down the street.

Chapter 8

After school, Rose stood on her side of the room using my new mirror to observe her form as she drew back with her bowstring.

Initially, I didn't like that she was using my mirror. But then I realized it might not be a bad idea to share. Maybe she'd see the strange things, too. And if she didn't …if she didn't hear the voices…it would confirm that I needed help.

"You ready to go see the movie?" I slipped on a purple sweater because it matched the stripes on my shirt.

"I thought we weren't going until later." Rose panted with a furrowed brow, struggling to maintain her form.

"Dad's taking us out to eat first." I said, starting toward the mirror, but stopped halfway. Rose needed time to witness the same things I'd gone through. Interruption was a sure way to prevention.

"Really?" She immediately began to disassemble her bow. In her haste, she grunted and grumbled and rolled into a tangled ball of body and bow. A laugh threatened to burst through my lips, so I cupped my hands over my mouth.

After a few minutes, I offered to help. Rose ignored

me, still struggling with de-stringing her bow. "Why don't you take that apart when we get back?"

Rose looked up from her tangled mess, clearly offended. "If I leave it here like this, it'll stress out the limbs! They'll grow weak! Then they won't work properly!" She threw her hands up dramatically. "You don't understand anything!"

I understand quite a lot. Like Rose can be a drama queen of epic proportions. And that she won't give up this archery thing even if it meant continuing would cause the amputation of at least one limb. "Okay. Okay!" I threw my arms into the air, too. "Fine. Take it apart."

"Thank you." She promptly returned to the everlasting battle with the bowstring. Once she got the string off, she disassembled the limbs. The first pulled off from the riser easily but the second one was stuck. Rose pulled and yanked but it was clearly a fight that she would lose. After what seemed like forever, she must have realized her predicament. "Okay. Fine." Rose tossed the mess on her bed. "It's de-strung. That's good enough for me!" She marched out of the room, her arms crossed.

"Ready to go?" Dad asked when we entered the family room.

"Yes," Rose grunted. If she was going to be a grump, I certainly didn't want her going with my friends. She'd just spoil all the fun.

I shrugged. "Yeah, I guess." I wouldn't allow her to ruin my good mood.

"Great. Pile up!" That was dad's *cool* way of instructing us to get into the car. After trying to explain to him that this was not at all cool or funny, I realized it was a losing battle.

We stopped by a sandwich shop on the way to the theater. Rose had a mushroom melt (what was with her mushroom obsession anyway?) and I ate pastrami on rye. When we arrived at the theatre, Dad pulled up to the curb. Cindy and her step sisters, Winnie and Bertha, were sitting on the bench outside with Scarlet.

I leapt out of the car, leaving Rose to close the door.

Dad rolled down his window. "Remember," he said, sticking his head out of the opening, "don't talk to strangers!"

"Da-ad!" I moaned. "You're embarrassing." What did he think we were? Toddlers?

Dad gave a disapproving look, rolled up the window, and drove off.

"I've been looking forward to this!" Rose said to Scarlet. It was probably her way of saying thanks.

"Me too!" Scarlet nodded with a wide grin. "It's going to be so cold!"

Cindy raised her eyebrow. "What do you mean?"

Scarlet looked at her with a furrowed brow, but her eyes widened as if suddenly remembering. "Oh! I mean, cool."

Cindy laughed. "Your new expression is totally cold!" She knew how to handle almost any situation.

"Thanks." Scarlet gave a thumbs up.

Winnie and Bertha giggled, using their hands to hide their mouths.

"Well, what are we waiting for? Come on!" I led the way inside the theatre, my backpack slung over my shoulder, loaded with contraband in the form of various candy. We found a seat in the very top row, cutting jokes and laughing. A man in a top hat sat in front of us, blocking my view. *Great. Who wears a top hat to the movies?*

The lights dimmed—and so did our laughter—and the movie started. We watched in awe, only reacting with jumps and gasps. But while my friends were engrossed in the film, I couldn't take my eyes off the man with the top hat. Mostly because that's all I could see.

By the time the movie ended it was getting dark. We dashed outside and sat on the bench while we waited for our rides. The top-hat man strolled past, whistling a weird tune. He tipped his hat at me with a wink and then climbed into a hearse.

A hearse! Who drives a hearse? Before I could point him out to my friends, Scarlet's parents chugged up in their little, old jalopy. I waved goodbye as Scarlet leapt into the vehicle, followed by Winnie and Bertha.

As they piled into the car, Cindy ran straight for me. "Thanks, Chickadee. I had a great time." She turned to leave then snapped back around. "Oh, and happy birthday!"

"Uh, me too," I said, not really paying much attention. I was too busy watching the man make loop-de-loops in the parking lot in his dead-body wagon.

"It was totally cold." Scarlet waved from the backseat.

"Best. Movie. Ever!" Winnie and Bertha shouted together.

Cindy sidled up next to Scarlet and buckled her seat belt. In a moment they were gone.

As soon as they were out of sight, the man in the hearse drove up to the curb and rolled down his window. "Sarah White," he called. "Do you know how to get to...?"

My jaw came unhinged. How did he know my name? I started to answer him, but Rose nudged me with her elbow. She whispered under her breath, "Don't talk to strangers."

"Well, I'm no stranger!" The man smiled so huge his teeth showed and I thought his eyes would pop out of his head. "After all, I do know your name."

"My...my...name?" The words stumbled out of my mouth.

"It's your birthday, isn't it, Sarah?" the man asked.

I nodded.

"Better be careful with reflections."

"Reflections?" I echoed the word in a whisper, feeling really creeped out because I had seen strange things in the mirror, and it was almost as if this weirdo knew about it. It was also the same warning Hunter had given me.

"Are you hearing voices, too?" he asked.

My eyes nearly popped out of my head. *How did he know?*

Steve: *Don't answer that.*

Creepy: *Heh-heh. Oh yessssss. Anssssswer him.*

Slimy: Sarah White, you're hearing voices. aren't you?
Creepy: Nah. It's just us. Heh-heh.
Steve: Listen to me. You don't want to answer him. Or them for that matter.

I'm not quite sure, but with my mouth agape, I think I nodded.

The man laughed then drove off. His strange chuckle clung to my ears long after he was out of sight.

Chapter 9

S ilence fell upon us like a heavy spring frost as we entered the house. Mom sat on the couch watching some dumb television show. She put her finger to her pursed lips. "Shhhh."

Rose and I tiptoed through the door. "Is Tommy sleeping?" I asked.

Mom nodded. "I put him to bed early. He's been tired lately."

"Oh." I slipped onto the couch next to Mom.

She patted my knee. "Did you enjoy the movie?"

I nodded, but my stomach churned at the thought of the strange man. He knew me by name. He knew about my mirror. He knew about the voices in my head. That was a little too stalkerish if you asked me. There's no way I could mention it to my mom, or she'd flip out. My heart beat wildly as I glanced at Rose. She better not say anything! I needed to get out of there fast. "Well, it's been a long day. I'm going to bed. Goodnight." I darted off, taking the stairs two at a time.

I wasn't in the room long and Rose entered. She grasped my shoulder, squeezing it tight. "You're not still upset about the man at the movies, are you?"

I swallowed hard and nodded.

"C'mon, it was nothing. Don't be upset over something so silly." She flopped down on her bed.

"Fine," I said, the uneasiness in my belly coming out in a burp.

Rose grabbed my hands, which I didn't realize were shaking. "So why are you trembling?"

"There's something I need to tell you." Don't ask me why I thought it was a smart move to confide in her but with the addition of the crazy man at the theatre, I felt like I might really lose it if I didn't tell someone.

"What is it?" She looked sincere as she added, "I'm all ears."

There was no easy way to say what I'd been thinking, so the only way to handle it was to blurt it out. "I think my mirror is haunted."

Rose smirked but stopped when she saw the sincere concern troubling my face. "Don't be stupid! Mirrors can't be haunted."

"But you heard that guy. He knew my name and—"

"Well, I think most adults can read, don't you?" She pointed to my backpack. Mom had written my name in black marker across the top.

That's how he knew my name! "But...he knew about my birthday..."

"I'm pretty sure someone wished you a happy birthday while we were out," she said with a shrug.

"He also knew about my mirror." I didn't dare mention how he'd also asked if I'd been hearing voices because I didn't want to discuss that. I was too scared that I'd lost my marbles.

"Because he warned you to be careful of reflections?" She jumped up from the bed, landing gracefully on both feet, and threw her hands into the air. "That could mean anything."

"Okay. Fine." I sighed. "Maybe it's not haunted. Maybe it's cursed."

"I don't believe you," she added, as she inched toward me, "and how could it be haunted? Give me one good reason why you think it is. And I'm not talking about that weird guy. We've already found reasonable explanations for that." She crossed her arms and tapped her foot impatiently.

"We still don't even know who sent it!" Irritated, I rolled my eyes. That didn't need explaining. She should have realized an anonymous gift was weird enough. "Take a look at this!" I grabbed her hands and shoved her in front of the mirror. Maybe she'd see the strange things it does. Then I wouldn't feel like something was wrong with me.

"Whoa. Scary," she said. "It's my reflection."

She was right. Her reflection was totes scary. "Listen, every time I look in the mirror, my reflection does something strange."

"That's because *you're* strange." She turned away from the mirror and furrowed a brow, the freckles across her nose blending into a tan line.

"Do you want to help me or not?" I heaved myself on the bed. "Because if not, then just go away."

"Fine. Tell me more about this strange mirror."

My lips were pursed, jaw tight.

"Oh c'mon. I promise I'll believe you." Rose sat next to

me and ran her fingers through my hair. The tension in my jaw relaxed.

"Just before I went to sleep last night," I started, hesitating to tell her more, but then I took a deep breath and continued, "it glowed." I rolled over to look her in the eyes, but she had a poker face. "And…"

"There's more?" Rose looked at me pensively.

"And it hums a creepy tune!" I blurted.

Her eyes widened, as if she was as weirded out by it as I was. "Oh. My. Gosh," she said.

I held back the tears of relief. She was sympathizing with me after I shared something personal and scary. I never thought I'd see the day!

"Oh my gosh," she repeated. "How creepy is that? I mean, you're right."

"I am?"

"Yes. Your mirror is cursed." She leapt off the bed and pointed to its shiny surface.

"It is?"

"Yes! It has to sing you to sleep!" she busted out laughing, slapping a hand to her knee. "That really is a curse!"

My throat burned with angry words that I choked back. I couldn't believe I fell for it. I'd never be able to trust her. "Ha. Ha. Very funny." Hot tears stung my eyes.

"Haunted mirror! Yeah, right!" She paused to look at me before adding, "You're not really crying about this, are you?"

I wiped away the tears. "You're obnoxious." If I wouldn't be grounded for it, I totally would have smacked her with my pillow. "And it *is* haunted."

"Fine. Prove it."

"I will." I took my phone from my backpack and set an alarm for eleven o'clock p.m. "Tonight we'll sit in front of the mirror. We'll watch it together."

"That's easy enough." Rose scrunched up part of her face. "And if I'm right?"

"Then I'll never bother you about this again."

"You swear?"

"Pinky promise."

She sighed and something about it told me I would regret ever asking her. "Fine." She threw her head back melodramatically. "Let me get into my pajamas and then we'll deal with this haaaauuunted mirror of yours."

Did she really have to mock me? "Great, thanks." My words were dripping with sarcasm.

Rose ignored me, grabbed her clothes from her dresser, and went into the bathroom to change.

"Just you wait—"

THUD! Rose slammed the door.

"You'll see! I'll prove it to you!"

Rose peeked out and cast a sideways glance at me.

"You won't regret this!"

"I better not." She rolled her eyes then slammed the door shut again.

While she changed, I wrapped a blanket around my shoulders and sat on the edge of my bed, staring at the mirror. "C'mon, c'mon, c'mon. Don't make me look stupid in front of my sister. Show your sparks of light and your strange reflections." I pulled the blanket tighter with a shiver. "We could do without the maniacal laughter though, if you don't mind."

#

Creepy: Oh, there'll be laughter allllll right.
Icky: *achoo!* Just as soon as I stop sneezing.
Stinky: But the light isn't from the mirror.
Slimy: It's from your noxious farts.
Steve: No it's not. The light is from the necklace.

"Are you talking to the mirror?" Rose shouted. The acoustics in the bathroom made her laughter echo way too loud. Why'd she insist on making me feel like an idiot? I sat up straighter, not letting her taunts get to me. My conviction was strong. This mirror was cursed. No one would convince me otherwise. A moment later the bathroom went dark and Rose shimmied her way onto my bed. "When is this *haunting* going to happen?"

I turned to face her and cleared my throat. "Later."

"How much later?"

"Errr...just before I fall asleep." I flinched waiting for her to punch me with her fist but when I didn't feel contact, I peeked out of one eye.

Rose groaned. "Well I'm not waiting all night."

"You won't have to." I shushed her and resumed staring at the mirror. If she'd only heard the voices, too, she'd know for sure. But I was beginning to think they really were only in my head making me crazy. And all I wanted was to be normal. "Be patient."

As the words left my lips a flash of light exploded in my room and then everything went dark.

Chapter 10

A beeping noise pulled me from sleep, and I noticed a horrible taste invading my mouth. My eyes fluttered open only to find Rose's foot lodged between my lips. My gag reflex kicked in and I pushed her foot away. "Gross." Last I'd heard, Mom said Rose had a bad case of athlete's foot. Now I was doomed to have athlete's mouth! What would happen if it spread? And it ended up all over my face? Ugh!

"What?" Rose moaned. "Let me sleep."

Sunlight poured in through my window. Oh no! I must have set my alarm for the wrong time! I glanced at the clock. It was already long past noon. "It's morning," I said. "Actually, it's already past lunch."

The lingering taste of Rose's foot made me gag again and I bolted to the bathroom holding back the bile that crept up my throat. "Time to get up," I said through a foamy mouthful of toothpaste. "Did you see anything last night?"

"Yeah. I did," Rose said. She sat up and her eyes lit with excitement.

I nearly choked on the minty paste. "Really?"

"Oh yeah."

"What did you see?" The toothpaste flew out of my

mouth, splattering on my reflection and clouding the mirror.

"My crazy sister." Rose yawned and stretched.

She was a real comedian. "Very funny."

"I thought you said you would leave me alone after last night." She finger-combed her hair and tied her red curls into a high ponytail.

I huffed. "Okay. You're right." The cap fumbled from my fingers as I struggled to twist it back onto the tube of toothpaste. "But just out of curiosity, did you really happen to see anything?"

Rose groaned loudly and shuffled out of the bedroom. I chased her down the stairs, nearly plummeting to my death on the last three steps.

"Everything okay?" Dad asked between puffs of air as he blew up a balloon. He tied off the end and added it to the growing pile on the floor.

"Yeah. Everything's just great." I tossed my hands into the air, frustrated.

"You seem..." he paused, taking another balloon from the package. "Frazzled."

"I'm fine." Avoiding further conversation, I marched into the kitchen for breakfast. Rose was already sitting at the table, shoving spoonfuls of sugar-coated cereal into her mouth. "Why do you have to be like that?" I pulled a box of cereal from the cupboard and slammed it onto the counter.

"Oh c'mon," Rose said as milk dribbled from her mouth. "You didn't really think you'd see anything, did you?"

Yeah, I kinda did. "No." I shrugged.

"If you wanted an elementary school sleepover with your cool big sister, all you had to do was say so."

That's what she thought it was? If I hadn't been so hurt and angry, I would have laughed. Instead, I turned to the fridge for the milk. As I shut the door, Tommy toddled into the room, thumb in mouth.

"Morning, Tommy." My salutation lacked its usual cheerfulness, even though I was glad to see him.

Tommy waved and hummed a tune. A creepy, eerie little tune.

"That!" I pointed to Tommy. "That's the song!"

Tommy said something, but with his thumb still in his mouth it was hard to understand.

"Where did you hear that tune?" My voice became urgent as I knelt in front of Tommy shaking his shoulders. "Did you learn that from my mirror?"

"Mirror," Tommy said with his thumb in his mouth.

"Oh, leave him alone," Rose groaned. "He probably heard it at preschool."

"Preschool!" A smile grew on Tommy's face and he jumped up and down enthusiastically. "Preschool."

"See. Just like any small child, he's only repeating the last word we say."

"Mirror," I said, testing Rose's theory.

But Tommy didn't respond this time, he just toddled out of the kitchen to the family room.

"I'm telling you, that's the same tune—"

"Drop it, Sarah. Please." Rose rubbed her forehead. "I'm so over this drama you create. Why can't you just be normal?"

Little did she know, that's all I really wanted. To be normal. I wanted to go back to the old me. To the one who woke up hours before school to beautify herself. The one who didn't hear voices and see strange things. Now I was a total freak just like her.

"Fine. It's done." Leaving my food untouched, I stormed to my room, making sure to bolt the door. There's no way she was coming in here just to bug me. After I threw on my clothes, I went to the bathroom to apply some make up but, I was distracted. All I could think about was my haunted mirror. "Just go over there. There's nothing wrong with it. It's just a mirror."

Mesmerized, I dropped my mascara in the sink and inched my way toward the birthday mirror. My reflection gazed back. I waved my hand and my reflection did the same. I pursed my lips and so did the likeness staring back at me.

It was just a mirror.

That's all it was. A stupid, uninteresting mirror with a reflection of a girl who just so happened to have a gigantic imagination.

Along with a bunch of voices in her head.

Voices she wished would disappear.

If the mirror wasn't haunted and all of that was my imagination, then what was wrong with Hunter? Why would he warn me to be careful with reflections? And why did that man with the top hat mention it, too?

I opened my jewelry box and found the pendant from Grandma Millie. Thankfully Rose hadn't taken it back yet. The clasp clicked as I fastened it around my neck. Finger-combing my hair, I stepped back and admired myself.

Rose banged on the door and I startled. "Let me in. Now!"

I turned the bolt and Rose barged in. She rifled through her drawers, grabbed an armful of clothes and stopped suddenly. She whipped her head in my direction, eyes falling on the necklace. "You!" She pointed at my throat. "You think you can just wear my stuff anytime you want?"

My fingers crawled to my neck until they found the pendant from Grandma Millie. I debated taking it off. Was it really worth making my sister so upset? But was it really so hard for her to share? "I...uh..."

"Fine." Rose gritted her teeth. "Be that way." She stormed out and her complaints carried up the stairs as she whined to Mom.

This was all too much. Rose and her drama. My strange birthday gift. Something had to give. *Let's start with the mirror,* I thought as I twiddled with my necklace. "Just my imagination. The mirror, the music, the voices, and the strange reflection. That's it. All just a figment of my overactive imagination."

Steve: Are you sure?

A flash of blue lit the room and I jumped out of my skin, jerking my hand away from my neck. "Who's there?"

Steve: I told you. My name is Steve.

"Stupid voices. Stupid, stupid voices," I mumbled, my heart thudding wildly as I realized something was very different about the reflection. My hands trembled as I reached up to my neck, realizing precisely what was wrong.

Grandma Millie's necklace was gone!

Chapter 11

I must have broken it when I jerked my hand away. Why do I have to be so jumpy?

My legs wobbled uncontrollably, and I dropped to my knees. "Oh no. No, no, no," I cried. "This can't be happening." Tears welled up in my eyes. "She'll kill me." A fire lit in my throat as I held back the tears.

This was a family heirloom. Completely irreplaceable. I needed to find it fast or there would be heck to pay. The heat kicked on and warm air blew into the room. That's it! I lifted the grate and stuck my arm into the vent and groped around. Nothing! My stomach sank like a bowling ball.

"No." My body trembled. "It can't be gone. It just can't." Why did this have to happen? Why'd Rose have to be such a drama queen? Why'd I insist on pressing her buttons?

Now I'd lost a family heirloom, and no one would ever forgive me. Then I'd be the outcast of the family. Just like my Uncle Phillip. The one who sent me the mirror for my birthday…This was all his fault!

What was I going to do now? And how would Rose handle it? Her wrath had the force of a thousand suns on a good day. If she ever found out I lost her necklace, I was a goner. Might as well call me the walking dead.

Through my tears, I talked to my reflection. "It couldn't have gone too far. It's got to be here somewhere. I'll find it." My face, stained with black mascara tears, looked a wreck. I got down on my knees in search of the necklace, but as I knelt, my reflection remained standing.

My heart gave one hard thud before stopping just like my breath.

Air. I needed air.

My skin prickled and tingled. The reflection pointed a long finger toward me. Oh no! I was coming after myself! The reflection smiled sharply.

"Sarah," Mom's voice called as she knocked on the door. She peeked in and when she saw me, she gasped. "Are you alright?"

I straightened my shirt, still feeling totally spooked. "I'm fine." But my voice said I was lying because it quivered.

Mom rushed over, opening her arms for a hug. I squirmed out of her grip. "You don't look fine." She tried to brush a strand of my hair behind my ear, but I ducked away. If she got too close, she might notice the goosebumps covering my skin. Then she might think I was sick and cancel my party. I rubbed my arms to make the bumps disappear.

"You're cold?" Her brow furrowed. "You must have a fever." She placed her hand on my forehead. "Maybe you're coming down with something. Oh no. Please don't say you're sick. I'd hate to cancel the party. What would we do with all the food we prepared? Oh, and little Tommy. You weren't around him this morning, were you?

You know how miserable he gets when he's sick and then what if—"

"Mom," I interrupted her. "It's fine. I'm not sick."

She nodded slowly, like she was in a daze. "Well, you better get ready," she said clearing her throat. "Your friends will be here any minute."

"Oh, that's right." I really did need to hurry. I'd totally forgotten the gang was coming early to help set up. "Okay, okay. I'm getting ready. See?" I clipped the birthday barrette into my hair.

"Wear this." Mom picked up a sweater and handed it to me.

I slipped it on. "Don't you have something to do?"

"I'm just admiring my beautiful daughter. Is that a crime?" Mom sighed with a smile as she watched me rub away the smeared mascara and apply a fresh coat.

A fresh coat of pink lip gloss finished off my look. "Get a casserole ready or something?"

"My casserole!" Her eyes grew huge and without another second of hesitation, she bolted down the stairs. "The casserole's going to burn," she shouted. "Alabaster, give me a hand. Quick!"

A few seconds later Dad stood in the doorway of my room, stroking his chin. "You're not ready yet." It sounded like a question because his voice went up at the end.

Huffing, I crossed my arms. "Well, if everyone would stop pestering—"

"Alabaster!" Mom's voice sounded through the floorboards.

Dad whipped his head toward the staircase. "I'll be right there."

As soon as he left, I slammed the door. Enough with the interruptions already! Turning to march back toward the mirror, I stumbled on Rose's archery equipment. Normally, I'd be angry, but a weird twang hit my gut. Rose's half of the room told a story of her one and only interest: archery. It was also strikingly clear that she ignored trends. She obviously didn't care what people thought about her. That archery was uncool. So why should I care if my hair wasn't perfect or my shoes didn't match my outfit? In some ways, I envied her ability to just ignore the naysayers

Creepy: Ennnnnvvvvyyyyy.
Steve: Stop that. You're going to scare her.
Creepy: But that'sssss my job.

The voices were back! No! This couldn't be happening. Not before my party.

"All right, Princess," Rose said, suddenly barging in our room. "Everyone's here and they're waiting on you."

"Coming," I said, feeling unsettled. The family room was flooded with balloons and a birthday banner stretched across the back wall of the room. Presents covered the entire coffee table.

"Happy birthday!" my family and friends shouted in a chorus of cheers.

My cheeks flushed. "Thanks guys."

Rose's jaw came unhinged as she stared at my neck. She had eyes like a hawk. I should have known she'd notice the missing necklace.

My face burned as my hand flew up to my throat. "Don't worry. I'll find it."

"You mean you lost it?" Rose asked with a gasp.

"Well...I...you see..." I fumbled over my own words. How could I explain this to her? She'd never forgive me.

"I'm waiting." Rose lunged forward. "And if you don't tell me," she held up a fist, threatening me with a knuckle sandwich, "you'll have this for your birthday dinner."

My face grew red with embarrassment. I couldn't believe my friends were about to witness my sudden death, courtesy of my sister Rose.

Chapter 12

Mom jumped in. "You lost the necklace? Sarah, how could you do such a thing? You know that's a family heirloom."

"I didn't *lose it*." My gaze fell to the floor as I rubbed my toes together. "I just misplaced it. But I'll find it! I promise."

"You better." Rose gritted her teeth. "Or there's going to be he—"

"Watch your language, young lady." Mom gave Rose her death-glare. "We'll settle this later."

"You can bet I will." Rose clenched her fists.

"Well, isn't it a nice afternoon for a party?" Dad said. "I mean…paaaar-taaay. Because that's what we're gonna do!" My dad tried to be cool, but he was so lame.

"Open dis un!" said Tom through his thumb filled mouth. He toddled over to the table and picked up a box wrapped in purple paper. He handed me the gift, while still managing to jump in place.

"Tommy picked it out all by himself," Mom said.

I unwrapped it, revealing a silk scarf in a lovely shade of sea foam green. It reminded me of the ocean, which made me long for another trip to the beach. "Thanks,

Tommy." I gave him a big squeeze then ruffled his curly hair. He smiled behind his thumb.

Presents were then heaved on me all at once.

"Open mine first," Hunter said, handing me a gift bag overflowing with pink tissue paper.

"It's from both of us," Ethan said.

I flung the tissue paper into the air and it fluttered softly to the floor. Reaching inside the bag, I pulled out a stuffed animal. A gray-furred Siberian husky—or maybe a wolf, it was hard to tell the difference. It had pretty blue eyes and squeaked when I squeezed it. A card was attached with a ribbon around its neck.

"Don't open the card now." Hunter's face grew tomato red. "Open it later."

"Oh, okay." I felt my cheeks blush, too.

"Here's mine." Cindy shoved a gift into my stomach. "Open it."

The elaborately embossed white paper was much too pretty to rip, so I carefully peeled away the tape. Underneath all the wrapping lay a beautiful wooden box. The top was engraved with trees. Their branches stretched until they reached the other side, twisting together in a rope-like fashion. A crow with beady eyes perched on a limb. Beneath the branches were a little cobblestone path. Chills swept down my spine. The carving was exactly like the one on my mirror.

"It's beautiful!" I stroked my fingers over the engraving, fighting the goosebumps that crept onto my arms. "Thank you."

"I worked really hard on it. Look," she held up a finger with a bandage. "Nearly cut it off with the Dremel."

"You mean you made this?" My jaw came unhinged. "How did you…" My heart stopped beating mid-sentence. If Cindy made the box, had she carved my mirror, too? Maybe this was all a great, big practical joke. An awkward grimace that pulled at my lips made me feel as sick as I imagined it looked.

"Well, not by myself." Cindy smoothed her fingers across the engraving. "Mr. Petto helped."

Of course! Mr. Petto was a woodworker. He'd taught shop class, too. But why would he send me a mirror?

"Open it!" Cindy tapped the lid.

"There's more?" My skin crawled. I didn't know if I could handle another surprise. Prying the lid open, I peeked inside. Velvet lining snuggled a key. I ran my finger over its golden shank before gripping it in my palm.

"A skeleton key," she said. "They open anything, you know."

I held it up, admiring it. "Does it work on the box?"

"Of course it does. You can lock away your treasures. Plus," she said, her face and tone brightening, "the key is a charm for the bracelet I gave you the other day."

"Really? Wow! That's so cool."

"Can I put it on for you?" As Cindy started to clip it onto my bracelet, I realized the key looked familiar.

"Isn't this the one you used to wear…"

She nodded. "I thought you might like it."

"I couldn't. This belongs to you. I know how special it is."

"Don't worry. It's not the original." Cindy held up her wrist. "I had a copy made at the hardware store for you."

She clipped the key onto my bracelet. "Besides, you'll need it for the box."

"Here." Scarlet interrupted.

"What's this?" I blinked.

Scarlet held out her hands. One held a bouquet of roses, the other an apple. "Mort told me it was tradition to bring fruit." She shrugged and I did too. The Small family had strange traditions.

"Thanks," I said taking the gifts.

Scarlet cleared her throat. "An apple a day to keep the doctor away. You're the apple of my eye." She gave an awkward laugh. "Don't upset the apple cart." Her voice trailed off in uncertainty with her weirdly inappropriate idioms.

"That's really nice of you, Scarlet." Even though I felt it was a bit odd to bring a piece of fruit as a gift, I did what any reasonable person would do. I took a gigantic bite of the juicy, red apple and smiled. "It's really sweet."

"I knew it would be perfect." A strange smile stretched across Scarlet's face. She looked like a crazy person.

"It's crisp and tarte, too. And—" Suddenly, a small piece of apple lodged in my throat.

Steve: Breathe, Sarah! You'll be okay.

Creepy: No, you won't. Don't listen to him. You're gonna diiii-ieeeeee.

Slimy: If she dies, I get first dibs on the hypothalamus. It's my favorite part.

    I coughed and sputtered. My breath hitched. The apple was poisoned! Reaching out, I grabbed Scarlet's red cape, her eyes darkening into solid black orbs. My so-called friend was trying to kill me!

Chapter 13

Dad flew at me, and Scarlet dodged out of the way. He banged his hand on my back. The chunk of apple shot across the room, narrowly missing Hunter's face. Air punched my lungs and I gasped. My head felt woozy from the lack of oxygen.

"That was a close one." Dad hugged me.

"Are you all right?" Mom asked.

I nodded. "I think so."

"Next time, try chewing your food," Dad joked.

"Sure. No problem." I feigned a smile.

"So how about you open one final gift?" Dad pushed a very large box across the living room floor. "This one's from us."

I opened the present, revealing a laser tag game for six people. What the heck? Did they mistake me for Rose?

"Whoa. That's probably the coolest gift ever," Hunter said taking a laser gun from the box.

"You think so?" I felt the heat in my cheeks fade.

"Absolutely." Hunter turned the laser toy over in his hand. "Let's play!"

Cindy grabbed my hand. "That's a great idea!"

"You in?" Hunter asked Scarlet.

"I suppose I could play a round," she said, growling and crossing her arms.

"Maybe we should help with clean up first." Cindy started collecting some paper cups.

"Don't worry about that. I've got it. You kids go have fun." Mom tipped her head in that way she does when she's pleased.

"Suck up," I mouthed to Cindy.

Creepy: Oh, how I loooooove to suck things up. Nice, soft brainsssss. Sluuuuurp them into my belly.

Icky: *achoo* Yes, just like warm chicken noodle soup.

Stinky: And then we can have a burping contest.

I rubbed my head, hoping the voices would stop.

"Are you sure?" Cindy asked.

"That's very nice of you," my mom said to Cindy. "But you're our guest."

"Yeah, only her children are slaves in this house," I joked.

"What's gotten into you lately?" Dad's brow furrowed with concern.

I wanted to say, *"About seven different voices."* But instead I said, "Nothing." Then I tugged Cindy, pulling her away from the clean-up.

Hunter tapped a foot as he peered around the corner and up the stairs. "Did you get anything else for your birthday? Something special from a relative, maybe?"

My mom's face lit up. "Oh heavens, yes! Wait until you see—"

"Hey, would you look at the time? It's getting late and we still have laser tag to play." I brushed past my mom as I lunged toward the unopened game.

"I'll grab the laser guns," Ethan said, not looking at me as I held the box in my arms. His eyes were fixed at the top of the staircase as he whispered to his brother.

"Yeah, great idea." Hunter seemed spaced out, too. Definitely acting funny. Maybe he knew about my mirror.

Rose pushed past me and plopped on the couch. "You do that. Losers." She placed her fingers on her forehead, making the letter 'L' and pouted.

"That's coming from the loser who can't even hit the target," I quipped back. "I bet I have better aim than you."

"Da-ad! Did you hear what she said to me?" Rose whined. When he didn't respond, she threw her hands into the air. "Whatever."

"Apologize to your sister," Dad said.

"Yeah, an apology would be nice," I shouted at her.

Dad wagged a finger at me. "I was talking to you."

"But..." My breath left in a violent puff of air as if I'd been punched in the gut.

"You heard your father." Mom picked up wrapping paper from the floor.

What was with everyone? It was *my* birthday and I being treated like a criminal. "But she started it."

Dad raised an eyebrow. "I'm waiting for an apology, not an excuse."

"Fine." I crossed my arms in defeat. Then I mumbled an apology under my breath.

Rose lifted her head with a smirk. "What was that? I couldn't quite hear you."

I cleared my throat and shouted, "Sorry! Okay? I'm sorry. Happy now?"

Rose's smirk grew until she had a half-moon smile on her face, revealing large, white teeth. "Not yet." She laughed. The sound was closer to a witch's cackle.

BRAIN FREEZE

Creepy: Eeeeeviiiiiiil. She'ssssss pure evillllllll.

I nodded in agreement to the voice in my head. Rose was evil!

Chapter 14

"Thank you, Sarah. That's quite enough." Dad chomped into a chip. "Now go on outside."

I threw my hands up. No one was going to address Rose's behavior? Whatever.

"Here." Scarlet interrupted again. She wasn't exactly in tune with social cues, but the distraction was a welcome relief. She handed us each a vest with a flashing target. "Put these on."

"I'll give you a head start." Hunter steadied his laser.

But I quickly aimed mine and his vest lit up with one blast from my laser beam. A strike.

"Whoa." Hunter stumbled backward. "I changed my mind. I want you on *my* team."

For the first time since Rose's antagonizing behavior, I smiled. "Okay. Me, you, and Scarlet against Cindy and Ethan"

"But that's three against two." Ethan pulled his vest on.

I aimed my laser at him. "Guess you better hide fast. I'll give you a head start." We burst through the front door and ran outside.

"Mom told me I have to play," Rose complained as she walked out onto the porch.

I huffed loudly. "You've got to be joking."

"Trust me," Rose said as she slipped her arms into her jacket. "It's the last thing I want to do."

"You can be on our team." Cindy tossed her the last vest. "Then it'll be fair."

Rose was such a lousy shot it'd be a terrible disadvantage for anyone that got stuck with her. I should have warned them, but I bit my tongue instead.

"Now that we have our teams," Hunter said, pulling the hem of my shirt until I backed up to his side of the lawn, "maybe we should lay down some ground rules."

"Good idea," Ethan said.

Once the rules were established, I raised my laser. "Are we ready?"

"I'm ready!" Scarlet shouted. She seemed a little too eager.

"You have ten seconds to hide." Hunter turned his back.

"C'mon! Let's go!" Cindy grabbed Ethan's sleeve and the two took off running toward the side of the house.

Hunter peered over his shoulder. When he saw me standing there he said, "What are you waiting for?"

"Well, what's our plan of defense?" I whispered.

"Oh right." Hunter scratched behind his ear. "I hadn't thought that far ahead."

"Shoot to kill." Scarlet smiled a wicked grin.

I gasped, stumbling back a step. "Say what?"

"I mean, aim for the target." Scarlet laughed.

Hunter's eyes flashed at me. "Run. I'll find you."

"Promise?" My heart skipped a beat and a smile tugged at the corner of my mouth.

"Yes." He clutched his laser gun in both hands.

Without hesitation, I took off at full speed. There was a set of bushes near the garage and I ducked down behind them.

"Quiet," Scarlet said.

"Holy heck." My hand bolted to my heart. "You scared the life out of me."

"You'll give us away." Scarlet's voice was smooth as silk. Her teeth were white as milk. They looked a little pointier than normal, but it must have just been my eyes deceiving me in the dark.

My breath still came in pants. "I didn't even see you there."

Scarlet smiled. "I'm good at hiding."

"Apparently so. You know, I am—"

"Shhh!" Scarlet stopped me mid-sentence and put her hand to my mouth.

Awkward.

"Did you hear that?" she asked.

I started to speak but Scarlet clamped her hand tighter against my mouth.

"Footsteps," she mouthed.

It was near impossible to hear anything over the rapid thudding of my heart, but I listened and finally heard it. Just like she said.

Nodding, Scarlet peeled her hand away. She peeked between the bushes. "Ethan."

"Wide open," I said, pointing at the target on his back that was just begging to be hit.

"You do it," Scarlet said.

I placed my laser gun between the branches and closed one eye, aiming at Ethan's back. His target lit up.

"I've been hit!" Ethan peered down at his vest. He lowered himself to the ground and pursed his lips when he saw us hiding in the bushes. "I could have guessed."

Scarlet's target suddenly lit up. I fired aimlessly trying to defend her.

Cindy stumbled over. "One down," she said, smiling at her success.

"Yeah, but we're down two already." Ethan dropped his laser.

My stray beams had struck Cindy's vest which now lit up. "Awh man."

"You've only got Kat-*miss* left," I said trying not to laugh. "This will be easy."

Cindy gave a disapproving half-smile as she grabbed Ethan's hand, glancing off into the horizon. Dusk tickled the treetops. "It's getting late." She gulped. "I really have to go."

"Yeah, me too. Got a text from Mort and Drac. They'll be here soon." Scarlet stood. "If you find Hunter," she said to me, "the two of you can tag-team. Then you'll win."

"Good idea." I gripped my laser tighter.

"I have a feeling he's still near the front of the house." Scarlet whispered.

"What makes—"

"Trust me," Scarlet interrupted. "Front steps. Go!" Then she took off, leaving her vest and laser gun behind.

Chapter 15

Shimmying past the bushes, I reached the staircase and knelt down. "Hunter," I whispered.

"Shhh!" Hunter hushed. "Rose is right there." Blasts shot out.

"You've got her!" I squealed.

Hunter's target flashed. "No. She got me. I can't believe it."

"Me either." I patted his shoulder. "She has such terrible aim."

"Well, you're the only one left," Hunter said, crawling out from under the stairs. "Take her out."

"Oh, I'll take her out all right." Maybe I was taking this competition a little too seriously, but I needed to avenge Hunter's loss. Scoping the yard for any sign of my foe, I stepped lightly.

My back was turned to the street and I slammed into something. My breath shot out in a giant whoosh of air. When I swirled around, I was face to face with none other than my sister.

"Tag her!" Hunter yelled from somewhere off to my side.

"You're going down," I said through clenched teeth.

"Not if I take you down first." Rose raised her laser and aimed it at my target.

I raised mine, too. All I had to do was press the button. I'd win. Game over. But my hand shook. I couldn't do it. Maybe because it was too easy. Or maybe because Rose intimidated me a little bit. But most of all, I didn't want to deal with her attitude if I won the game. I'd never hear the end of it. Letting her win would be even easier…

"C'mon Sarah! You've got this in the bag!" Hunter walked into my line of sight. "Do it already."

"Stay out of this," Rose said. "This is between me and my sister." She flicked the tip of her laser for emphasis. "Hit my target now or I'm going to take you down."

"Fine." My finger trembled over the button.

"Are you going to do it or what?" Rose's eyes narrowed.

"Or what?" I repeated.

Rose pressed the laser's button, but she missed my target. "That was my first warning."

"Run!" Hunter called, snapping me from my thoughts. "Run now, Sarah!"

With a twist of my upper body, I knocked Rose's laser from her hand. I darted up the porch steps and ran straight inside the house.

I didn't stop until I reached the top of the stairs. With my laser at the ready, I backed into my room, bracing against the doorway.

This was no good. There needed to be a strategy. If I hid under my bed, she'd probably know to look for me there. My closet? Too predictable. Maybe I could hide under *her* bed...It was the perfect plan. I tiptoed toward her bed but stopped when I heard Rose's laughter.

Rose burst through the door. "You're cornered." She laughed, holding her laser steady.

She was right. There was no way out.

Rose inched forward and I raised my laser, aiming it at her target. "You're going to pay."

"Pay for what?" I trembled.

"You know what for." Rose's face scrunched up. "Don't act like you don't know."

She was still mad about the necklace. She'd never let it go. Out of the corner of my eye, I saw a small flash of blue come from under my dresser. Rose's necklace! Perfect timing! All I needed to do was grab it. Then I could give it to her, and all would be forgiven.

I fell to my knees and shoved my arm under the furniture. A rusty nail, sticking up from the floorboards, scraped my arm. "Ouch!"

"What are you doing?" Rose growled.

"I found it! Look!" Standing suddenly, I jerked the necklace up to eye level. It dangled from my fingertips, glowing a soft shade of blue. But another color bounced off the walls. Red, as bright as a stop light. Rose had finally done it. I stumbled backward, tripping over my feet. A feeling of betrayal sank in my stomach. "You shot my target?"

Rose's face was screwed up tight. "You bet I did." The necklace flashed again, sending beams of blue against the walls. Her expression softened. "My necklace! You found it!" She lunged forward, knocking into me and I teetered backward.

Hunter came rushing in. "Be careful of reflections," he yelled, racing over. He reached for my hand but, it was too late.

My head slammed against the mirror. Hard. Stars flashed before my eyes. The cold feel of glass touched my shoulder. Tingles pricked my skin, like ice cubes and thorny briars. A strange sensation crept from head to toe.

And then I fell.

Chapter 16

Blackness surrounded me as I passed through something cold, my skin both burning and freezing at the same time. One final breath hitched in my throat and I gasped. A moment later it was over, like it never even happened. "That was so strange. It's almost like I fell into an icy pond."

Rose and Hunter stood with their mouths agape.

"What's wrong with you two?" Goosebumps rose up on my arms. Hairs stood on end.

My sister squinted.

I threw my arms into the air. "I surrender, Rose. You win. Happy now?"

Hunter turned and the two started talking, but I couldn't hear them.

"Hey, what's going on? This isn't funny." Even though they were right in front of me, I felt so removed from them. Like they weren't even paying attention to anything I said. "Don't ignore me!"

Rose stared straight ahead. Her mouth formed into a circle as she pinched her eyes closed. Hunter threw his hands over his ears. Why couldn't I hear her scream? Had the fall caused me to lose my senses? Maybe I had a concussion.

Hunter pushed past Rose, who blinked and shook her head. He was just within my grasp but when I reached out to him, an icy surface blocked our contact. Hunter banged his hands on an invisible surface between us.

"I don't like this game anymore. Can we stop playing now? Let's go eat some leftover cake."

Tears streamed down Rose's face and she fell to her knees, pulling the hair on either side of her head.

"Sarah, Sarah!" Hunter's voice came in a soft whisper, which didn't match his concerned expression. His fists made contact with the surface in front of him as he pounded against it.

"It's okay. I'm right here." I reached out, trying to comfort him, but wondered why we couldn't hear each other.

Rose continued to weep. I'd never seen her so upset. Hunter knelt at her side and put his arm around her shoulder. She fell into him, leaning against his chest. He squeezed her in a hug and rested his chin on top of her head. After a moment, he looked angry as he slowly rose to his feet with his fists clenched. He kept his head lowered, then bolted out of the room.

When he returned, he brought my parents with him. They looked confused.

My mom approached. "Sarah?" she mouthed. "Sarah, if you can hear me," her lips moved fast and it was hard to be sure of what she was saying, "stay put. Don't move."

"Everything is going to be okay," Dad said. His quiet voice had that unintentional fake sounding promise. I knew it by the waver in his tone, a false sense of confidence.

"But I'm okay," I said.

BRAIN FREEZE

Creepy: No you're nooooot. You'll neveeeer be okaaaaaay.
Steve: Stop it. You're not helping the situation.
Crawly: They'll never find you. Heh-heh.
*Stinky: *sips drink* Yup. You'll be lost forever.*
Yucky: Don't you think we should have warned her the mirror was bad?

"If you can hear us...if you can see us..." Dad shook his head. Anxiety pulled at his eyes making them droop. "We'll get help and be back for you."

Mom and Dad helped Rose to her feet. The three of them shuffled out of the room.

"Where are you going?" I screamed.

Rose glanced over her shoulder, mouthing the words, "I'm sorry, Sarah."

I took a step back, gasping.

Rose was sorry? Was this some sort of alternate reality?

Hunter placed his hands on the invisible surface in front of him. "I'll find you," he said, his forehead wrinkled with worry. I longed to see his smile instead. "I promise I'll find you."

"But I'm right here." My voice choked off, burning through tears.

Hunter turned away and my heart sank.

"Where are you going?" I screamed. "Don't leave me!"

It was as if he heard my screams because he stopped in his tracks. "Sarah? Are you there?" He pressed his arm against the invisible surface and leaned his head into the crook of his elbow. His eyes changed, narrowing into thin slits and glowing a sickly yellow color. "Run, Sarah. RUN," he growled.

AHHH! I stumbled backward. "What's wrong with you?"

"Get out!" This time it was no doubt he shouted because the sound pierced my skull.

My legs wobbled as I inched away trying to create distance between us. "Out of where? How?" This was all so confusing. We were just playing laser tag and now it seemed like there was a world between us. "What are you talking about?"

"You've fallen through the mirror, Sarah." Hunter banged on the surface in front of him, which if he was right and this wasn't a joke, was the glass of the mirror.

I gasped. "How can that be? It's impossible."

"Reflections." Hunter shook his head. "Get out now!"

Panic choked me. "Okay." I stumbled back, back, back. My foot caught on something and I jerked it away, losing my balance and falling.

"Aaaaahhhhh!!" Cold air whooshed past me and I struck out, groping for anything that would stop my fall. Branches and twigs tore at me. My arms burned with the fresh scratches and scrapes. "Help!" I called, still falling down what seemed like an endless abyss. My heart thudded in my chest. I was too young to die! My twelfth birthday couldn't be my last!

The necklace began to glow, lighting my fall. I spied a ledge, which quickly approached with my rapid descent. If I landed on it without first bracing myself, it would be as if I'd fallen to my death from a ten-story building. I reached for a branch and the necklace started to dim. "C'mon," I cried. "Keep glowing."

The necklace brightened just as the branch scraped my face. I swiped at the twig, grabbing it between my fingers. My body jerked hard as it smashed against the wall, my arm nearly tearing from its socket. I screamed in agony but held on tight despite the pain.

Dangling perilously from my fingertips, the fire in my arm warned that it wouldn't hold out much longer. Swinging my body was the only way out of this situation.

My foot made contact with the ledge. Almost there! Loosening my grip on the twig, I slid down until both feet were firmly planted. "That was a close one," I said as I fastened the glowing jewelry around my neck.

Then its light faded, and everything went dark.

Chapter 17

"**N**o, no, no!" I slowly crouched down until I was sitting on the ledge, my arms hugging my knees, while I fought back tears. "This can't be happening. It's dark and I don't know where I am."

BRAIN FREEZE

Steve: You're going to be okay.

Tears streaked my face and I mopped them up with my sleeve. "You're okay. Be strong." Cautiously, I felt around. My hand hit something sharp. "Ouch!" I cried, but then quickly clamped my other hand over my mouth. There was no need to alert anyone of my presence. When the pain subsided, I crawled forward only to be struck on my cheek. "Ow, ow, ow. That narrowly missed my eye!" As I pulled the thorny vine off my face, my hands burned with new cuts.

Blowing on my hands to ease the pain, I collected my thoughts. I had to get home, back to my friends, my family, and my birthday celebration. I couldn't see five inches in front of my face, let alone the end of this darkness, but there had to be a way out. Walls closed in around me as I crawled forward.

The cold, hard ground made my body ache, but at least I wasn't in a free-fall anymore. Inching my way through the tunnel, a rock lodged itself in my knee. I groped around for the culprit. Once I found it, I squeezed it hard, willing it to turn to mush. My hands ached and so did my heart. "Stupid rock," I said as I pitched it into the darkness. The rock made a soft thud and I realized just how tiny this space was.

Suddenly panic stricken with claustrophobia, a bead of sweat formed on my brow and my heart thumped rapidly. Air. I needed air. I had to get out of here! I wiggled and writhed my way forward on my belly. Something crawled over my hand. The necklace began to glow, and I saw the creature sitting just inches away. A cross between a squirrel and a raccoon stared at me, it's beady eyes glowing red. Patches of fur covered its long body and its mouth frothed with white foam.

"RABIES!" I shrieked again and swatted it away. The creature yipped before scurrying off into the darkness. Maybe the fall didn't kill me, but disease surely would! Flopping on the ground in a heap of snot and tears, I was ready to give up. No one knew where I was, including me.

Deep breaths. As soon as my heart stopped feeling like a rabbit cornered by a lawnmower, I continued forward. A pinhole of light ahead promised hope. An exit! I rubbed my eyes. Could it really be?

"Light!" A joyful anticipation burned my chest as bad as Grandma Millie's five alarm chili-pepper stew. I scuttled forward crawling as fast as the tiny space—and my exhausted body—would allow.

With each inch, I thought of my parents and Hunter. I thought about Cindy and Scarlet, and yes, even Rose. They must be so worried.

"Don't give up," a voice whispered.

Stupid voices. They would never leave me alone. "Go away. You've bothered me for too long."

"Have it your way then," the voice said.

The light from my necklace glowed so bright it illuminated my surroundings like a midday sun. Ahead, the tunnel widened, and I could finally stand. The path forked off into two other directions. But I noticed something else. Surrounding me weren't vines, but skeleton hands! All those scratches I'd received weren't from thorns. They were from BONES!

A scream burst through my mouth, and the light from Grandma Millie's necklace pulsed, making a strobe effect as it bounced off the walls. "What the...what?"

"Calm down," the voice instructed. "It's a charm. Tells you when danger is near. Now relax and listen up."

"Who—who's there?" My voice trembled but I didn't care. I was entitled to feeling scared. After all, my crazy, haunted, weirdo mirror had apparently *swallowed* me, and I had no idea how to get home. My necklace glowed, and, unless this was another hallucination, there was a disembodied voice giving me instructions.

"Down here," the voice said. "The Living. Always with the questions," it mumbled.

My eyes fell on a small, white creature a few inches away from my hands. "Awww. What a cute little..."

"Mouse." The creature scurried forward.

"Ska-ska-skeleton mouse!" I screamed.

"As if I haven't heard that one before." He twitched his tail. "Cheddar. C-H-E-D-D-A-R," he announced with a humpf. "And not the cheese. Definitely not to be confused with Chester. I hate that name."

"Che…che…Cheddar?"

"Yes. Cheddar." He grunted, clearly bothered. "The Living. They all have hearing problems."

"What?"

"See what I mean?" His body made a clattering noise as he laughed with a grumpy sound. Who knew a laugh could be grumpy?

My necklace flashed a bright blue light as a flapping noise sounded in the distance.

"What's that?" Something flew toward me. It looked like a mosquito. I squinted and the mosquito grew bigger. My eyes widened as I realized it wasn't a bug. "A bat!" The creature flew in my direction and I ducked, covering my head with my hands. The bat landed in my hair, tangling itself in my beautiful curls. "Get it off, get it off, get it off!"

Cheddar marched up my arm, straight to my head.

"Ahhhhhh!" I shrieked.

"Hold still, would you?"

"What are you doing?" My head throbbed from the fresh wounds, bloated like roadkill.

"I'm trying to free my friend, Shade."

"What...er...who's that?"

"It's the bat trapped in your hair." The mouse harrumphed. "You really shouldn't use so much hairspray."

"Bat." I nearly fainted. "Hairspray?"

"Yes, now hold still. This might hurt a bit." A clump of hair ripped from my skull as the bat escaped my tresses. "See you soon, Shade!"

"Ahhhhh!" I swatted the mouse away and Cheddar skidded across the cave. In the distance, the freed bat made some weird high-pitched noise. I sucked in a deep breath, and bit my lip, trying not to shiver.

"I would appreciate it if you would stop trying to kill me." Cheddar panted. "That's happened once already. Not the most pleasant experience and I certainly don't want to do it again."

"What..." I mumbled, still trying to recover from the recent trauma. Bat hair was definitely worse than bed head!

"Can't you say anything else?"

"Uh…uh…" I groaned.

"Well, that's a start." He humpfed a really loud humpf, then lifted my head by pulling a few strands of my hair. "Now look out there."

My eyes fell on the light at the end of the tunnel. "I'm looking. All I see is light filtering between those creepy vines."

"Good. Now pull yourself together and get moving."

"Uhhh…okay." I gulped. "But…what's out there?"

"No need for that now. Just get on your knees, chop away at those vines and make your escape."

"But what if…."

The mouse folded his arms. "Now. Are you going to listen to me or are you going to sit there quaking like a bag of popcorn in the microwave?" His head jerked back, looking behind me into the depths of the unknown tunnel.

"What's the matter—"

"Just go!"

The necklace glowed and pulsed erratically. A warning. Just like Cheddar had said. I managed to turn enough to peer back over my shoulder. A very large shadow obstructed the tunnel.

Chapter 18

"What—what is that?"

Cheddar humpfed. A hurried, concerned humpf, but it was still a humpf. "Do you really want to find out?"

"Good point." Skeleton weeds rained down as I jerked them free from the opening. They clattered as they landed on the ground. Progress was slow and the shadow creature made steady gains. "Help me, Cheddar," I begged. "Please."

"The Living. Always needing help." Cheddar climbed up my arm and I shivered. He stood on my head and broke through a vine. "This isn't easy, you know."

"It's not exactly fun for me either." My nails were caked with dirt and my palms were raw with wounds. What would people think of me if they saw me now? I desperately needed a manicure. And maybe a doctor.

"You got that right. I could have chipped a tooth." His teeth clanged as they made contact with another skeleton vine.

Footsteps approached and my heart lunged. "Hurry."

"Almost there." Cheddar's grunt told me that he was as exhausted as I was.

Broken boney vines scraped my palms and blood dripped onto the earth. The bracelet Cindy gave me jingled and I wished the key had sharp blades like a saw. That would have really helped. "Just a little bit more." My breath came fast and heavy as fatigue and fear crept in.

"No need for a blow by blow," Cheddar scolded. "Don't you think I can see?"

I wasn't exactly sure. He was a skeleton, after all.

"Don't answer that," he said, as if he knew what I was thinking.

Only one vine stood between me and freedom. And only a few inches remained between me and the creature at my back. I had to get out before it grabbed me first.

Desperate, I pulled the vines. I tugged hard. "It's not working!" My throat ran as dry as a brook in the heat of a summer drought.

Cheddar peered back. "Hurry! It's close."

What he didn't say, but what I was able to interpret was, "And it might be too late."

No. No. NO! I so desperately wanted all of this to be a bad dream. Heck, I'd even settle for a head injury at this point. That was a real possibility. Maybe I had a concussion. If so, I was going to wake up and everything would be fine. "Wake up. Wake up. Wake up." I slapped my hand on my arm and pinched my skin.

"You're awake."

"That's what I was afraid of. So, I'm not dreaming?"

"Nope. But it's definitely your worst nightmare." Cheddar pawed at my hair. "If you don't hurry, you're headed on a one-way trip to a very deep sleep, permanently."

"What does that mean? You know what. Don't answer that. I don't want to know." Reaching the opening, I pulled the last and final vine, and my hand burst through to the other side. "I made it!"

But whatever was behind me cackled a shrill little laugh. And then it grabbed my ankle. Sharp blades dug into my skin. Hot streaks of pain shot up my leg and I let out a piercing scream. "No!" I kicked fast and hard, hoping to make contact with the creature and knock it out cold.

"Go." Cheddar scurried toward the creature and it let go of my leg.

Without a second of hesitation, I scrambled out of the enormous cave, falling a few feet to the ground. I landed in a patch of briars, feeling the burn on my face and the other exposed portions of skin.

"I made it," I whispered, not lifting my head. I couldn't. The thorns pulled me down, threatening to tear my flesh. "Jump out. I'll catch you," I called to Cheddar even though I couldn't move. That cranky, little mouse needed to escape. He just had to be okay.

A small yelp was followed by the clatter of bones.

"Cheddar!" I gasped.

Another cry and a crunch.

My heart sank. A sense of guilt—and gratitude—filled my chest. That mouse sacrificed himself for me. We'd only just met, too. I wasn't sure I'd do that sort of thing for my friends and we'd known each other forever. I certainly wouldn't have done something like that for my sister, Rose, and we'd known each other forever plus infinity. My new friend was gone, and I'd never see him again. I never even had the chance to thank him.

Briar's clawed at my skin as I clambered to my feet. I looked back at from where I'd fallen. Some sort of hole in a hillside, covered in vines and briars. Ahead of me was a foreboding forest, with creepy trees arching across a cobblestone bath. Just like my mirror! And the box from Cindy. I gulped.

My body burning in pain, and eyes welling with tears, I stifled the sob building in my chest. I couldn't allow myself to cry. I'd been through so much that it would be understandable if I did, but I couldn't break down and lose it again. No excuses, I had to be strong. That was the only way I was going to find answers. My mirror had transported me to another dimension but first I had to find out where I was.

"I'm not crying anymore. No more. No matter what." I cleared my throat.

"No more," a strange echo sounded.

"What was that?" My head jerked left to right, searching for the sound.

"What was that?" the echo said.

I looked up to see a bird situated on a branch of a leafless tree.

"Koww!" it cawed, fluffing its wings. Feathers floated down and pelted my head like rocks.

"Hey!" I shouted at the bird.

It cocked its head before cawing once more and flying off. It joined more crows on other leaf-less branches further ahead in the forest. I rubbed the back of my head where an especially heavy feather had hit me.

"Stupid bird." I picked up a white rock and shook it in

the air, threatening the crow. "How would you like it if I —" A gnawing in my gut stopped me mid-sentence and I peeled back my fingers. My hand trembled as I realized what I was holding.

A bone.

Chapter 19

"AAAHHHHHH!" I screamed.

"CAW!" The murder of crows screeched in unison. "Caw, koww, koww!" They flapped their wings as they broke out into a chorus of laughter.

"Why do you think that's funny?" My hands flew to my hips in defense. "It's hilarious that I picked up a bone. I bet you think it's hysterical that I screamed, too, huh?" I shifted my weight from foot to foot, throwing my hip from side to side.

"Scream," a bird called. "Scream. Scream."

A trio flew down, landing on a branch just above my head. Their black feathers shined with a glossy glow. "Scream. Scream. Scream."

This sounded like a command. "No. I'm not going to scream." Who did they think they were, bossing me around?

"Scream. Scream. Scream." The birds' wings rose as their heads sank lower, their command growing more and more menacing. I'd never seen a bird narrow its eyes before, but their eyes thinned into slits. Their beaks inched closer, making their body language even more threatening. "SCREAM!"

"Aaaah!!!" I stumbled and landed on my butt.

"Caw, koww, koww!" They cackled together.

These birds were grating on my last good nerve. "You really should mind your manners. It's not polite to laugh when someone falls." I wagged my finger at them just like my mom did when she was scolding Tommy. Oh no! Don't tell me that on top of the worst day in the history of worst days ever, I was turning into my mom! Of all things! "You are very rude birds."

"CAW!" the trio shouted together. One bird nodded and together they leaned forward, their claws digging into the branch. "Caw. Koww. Koww!" Then the entire murder of crows suddenly took off into flight, their feathers raining down and pummeling my head. Dad always told me if birds had erratic behavior, it was most likely due to a threat.

A loud rumbling noise marched up my spine, chilling me to the bone. I suddenly realized the birds had sensed it before I heard it and that's why they'd scattered, filling the sky like ashes from a fire. The rumble came again, and I stared at the tunnel, watching it tremble like a Jello mold in the hands of a clumsy waitress. I had a feeling that whatever was in the tunnel was about to make its appearance. No way was I sticking around to find out what it was.

"I'm outta here," I said, as I darted away from the tunnel. Vines on the hillside began to grow. They crept toward me, inching closer and closer. One of them wrapped around my ankle. "So much nope!" I struggled free, shaking it off.

Run, legs. RUN! I never considered myself fast, but I found some sort of supersonic speed buried deep in my gut. My legs burned. My chest ached. Good thing, too, because the tunnel crumbled like dominos spilling into the forest, close on my heels. The trees folded in on the dirt path, crashing into each other. As the trees collided, they made horrible groaning noises. Vines slithered along the ground, as I desperately tried to outrun them. My toe rammed into a rock and when I fell, my face slammed into the earth. The ground punched the breath from my lungs.

A caw sounded in the trees. The bird's wings created a breeze as he swooped down and clawed at my hair. I swatted him away. "Stupid bird. Can't you see I'm in enough trouble? I don't need you making matters worse!"

A vine found my ankle and snaked around it. Pulling me backward into the closing forest, the tunnel seemed to open. It was as if the vine were a tongue and I was headed into a mouth which was ready to swallow me whole. I was nothing more than an insect for this Venus fly trap!

I reached for my ankle, but the crow dove at my head.

"Go away!" I swatted at the bird as the vine sucked me further into the dark forest. Digging my nails into the dirt, I fought my way back. A sharp pain suddenly pricked my ankle and I turned around to see a crow biting at my skin. "Get lost! I'm in enough trouble without you trying to peck me to death."

"Caw!" The vine snapped off and I was free.

I stared at the bird confused. "You were trying to help?"

The crow sailed over head, and I leapt to my feet determined to keep pace as he led the way. "Wait," I yelled, as a thorny briar swatted my cheek, drawing blood. Legs weakened from exhaustion a sense of dread and desperation overtook me. "I can't do it."

"Caw!" The crow flew off, leaving me to fend for myself. He returned with a large murder of crows. They grabbed at my clothes. They pecked at my skin. My body grew weak and my vision went dark.

Chapter 20

A violent thunder clap followed by a loud cry brought me back into consciousness.

My eyes shot open. Dozens of inky black wings brushed my skin. The tiny talons of the crows clutched at my clothes. As I tried to wiggle from their grasp, I realized I wasn't on the ground. No, I was in the sky. The birds were helping me escape the forest. They'd worked together to lift me into the air, and fly above the treetops.

Another clap of thunder and feathers exploded near my ear. A crow's carcass tumbled from the sky to the earth below. A branch hit a bird before striking me in the face. The trees tore another bird from the sky. It plummeted to the earth in a loud splat. Then another bird and another. Something was taking the birds down, one by one.

A heavy sadness sunk in my chest. These crows were sacrificing their lives. Why would they do that? They didn't even know me.

"Caw!" One crow remained and he struggled to fly as we dipped and swerved with each strike of a tree branch.

"Hurry," I said. "Please hurry."

"Koww!"

"Sorry." I muttered. "I know you're trying. But..." I paused. "Any chance you can try—"

A branch pummeled toward us, smacking into my upper thigh. The bird lost his grip and I crashed to the ground. The air punched out of my lungs and I sucked in sharply. The trees were still hot on my trail and I scrambled to my feet. The crow was nowhere to be seen so I was on my own. I couldn't believe how many creatures sacrificed their life for mine. What kind of place was this that animals did such things? Speaking of oddities, what kind of place had a forest that tried to kill its trespassers?

With a renewed strength, my feet pounded the soil. In the distance a field of beautiful green grass dotted with flowers promised refuge on the other side. A lavender sky with billowing clouds beckoned to me. I pushed with all my strength, pumped my legs as fast as they would go. The opening was just a few feet away. I could make it. I had to.

As I was about to leap from the forest, a briar swatted and caught onto my clothes. It began to pull me back into the mouth of the forest. Kicking free, I threw myself onto the safety of the meadow's grass. The forest closed in with a loud groan. It collapsed and then sucked itself into the earth. "Whoa!"

My heart lurched. I'd escaped.

Then, exhausted, I collapsed face first in the grass. The ground sunk beneath me like a giant pillow. Cuts and bruises made my skin burn but I was so relieved to be free from danger that I barely noticed. A bug scuttled over, snapping its pinchers on my nose.

"Gross." I flicked it away. The bug shook a fist at me

before it burrowed into the ground and disappeared. "Phew. Glad that's gone."

Steve: Don't get too comfortable.
Creepy: Yeaaaaahhhhh.
Crawly: She's about to find out why. Heh-heh.

"You're still here?" I had thought those voices were a thing of the past. "Please...just...just go away."

A squirming under my belly made me laugh and I rolled onto my back. Inches from my face was something round. I turned it over. An eyeball!

The eye rolled into the rubber edge of my shoe as I screeched at the top of my lungs. It shot across the field as my foot made contact with it. Eyes pinged up from the meadow, like an arcade game.

My body shivered with the heebie-jeebies. I hadn't been laying in normal grass. Oh no, I'd been laying on a field of EYEBALLS! Nausea punched my gut, bringing me to my knees. "What kind of sicko puts eyeballs in a field? Huh? That's not what they mean by 'keeping an eye on things'!"

A gazillion thoughts entered my mind.

Maybe something *was* watching me.

Worse, I might be trapped in this strange world forever. I couldn't let that happen. There had to be a way out. The forest would be a suicide mission. Even if I could go back that way, it would be impossible since it had closed itself off.

The eye-field seemed less foreboding than the forest, even if it was a bit odd...and disgusting. Maybe it wasn't so bad if I continued in this direction. I'd already faced some pretty horrific unknowns. It certainly couldn't get any worse.

"CAW!" A large black crow flew overhead. He looked no worse for wear.

"I'm so glad you're okay."

"Stupid bird," it called.

My face grew hot. If only I'd known that he was trying to help me, I wouldn't have been so mean. "I'm sorry." I bowed my head in shame.

"Stupid bird," it crowed.

"I know. I get it. I called you stupid. I didn't mean it."

"Koww!" He flew off toward the forest. Now why would he go in that direction? He wouldn't even be able to get inside. What remained was barricaded with briars, vines, and tree limbs. The rest of it had been sucked into the earth. Fortunately for me, I wasn't curious enough to find out. I was smart enough to know not to go back there so I shrugged and kept walking, hoping the path would lead me to my family, and my friends.

A warm, sugary scent punched my nostrils. "Wow." I breathed. "That smells so good." I took another deep sniff. "Smells like....cotton candy!"

That treat brought back memories of the elementary school fall fun fair. Giddiness welled up inside until it overflowed and bubbled out, bringing a skip to my step. Making my way through the eye-field, I was greeted by an equally beautiful and creepy sight. A huge carnival loomed in the near distance, the Ferris wheel peeking out over the treetops. Red and white striped circus tents dotted the horizon. Sprinting toward the carnival I thought of all the yummy food. Fried dough. Hamburgers and French fries. And kettle corn. I chuckled thinking about Scarlet who called it Colonial Corn.

My stomach grumbled and my mouth watered as the smell and thought of food grew stronger. I would stuff myself with every last bite, then I'd wash it all down with a giant lemonade. I rubbed my belly realizing how very hungry I was. I'd been through a lot and it had been hours since I'd last eaten. Actually, it was near impossible to know how long it had really been. Maybe it was days. It sure felt like it.

As I approached the carnival a clownish man walked my way. A goofy grin pasted on his paper white face made me feel a tad bit uncomfortable. Okay, it made me a LOT uncomfortable because I have a fear of clowns, just like my BFF, Cindy. Coulrophobia is a real thing. Don't judge me.

The clown's smile grew sinister. "Where do you think you're going?"

My necklace strobed a bright white light, warning me of trouble.

Chapter 21

"Tt...ttt...tto the cc..cc..carnival," I stuttered.

"You can't go there just yet, silly!" he said as he giggled, in his creepy clown-giggling way.

The hairs stood up on the back of my neck. He had those crazy eyes. The ones that were icy cold and bugged out when they stared at you. "Uh. I mean, right, of course, I can't."

"My name is D," he said, sticking out a gloved hand. A pungent smell struck my nostrils and I wanted to barf. There was no way I wanted to shake his hand. Plus, my necklace was still strobing. Something smelled fishy about this and it wasn't just his disgusting dirt-caked glove.

Still, he was the first person I'd come across, so I gripped his hand tight. "D. Is that a nickname?"

"You mean you don't like it?"

Attention Will Robinson! Approaching dangerous territory. "Uh...no, no! D is a great name!" Where's a smile emoji when you need it? Quick. Subject change. "Have you seen my family?"

"Maybe!" He placed his white-gloved hand near his mouth as he giggled a full shoulder-shrugging laugh. "What do they look like?"

"Well, I've got a mom and a dad. And a little brother named Tommy. He sucks his thumb a lot."

The man laughed again.

Was it really that funny?

"And a sister named Rose. She has curly red hair." I paused before adding, "And she hates me." She cried pretty hard though when she saw the mirror swallow me, so maybe that wasn't true anymore. I shrugged and kicked my toes. "Or at least she used to."

The man stroked his chin as if he had a beard. Then he giggled and his bloated belly shook. Maybe this was a nervous habit. No one who was normal laughed that much. Especially not at the things I was saying. Even when I tried to crack jokes, I wasn't really that funny.

"Anyone else?" the man asked, his voice going up high on the end.

"Actually, yeah. My two best friends. I bet they're looking for me." A small ray of hope brought a smile on my face.

"Looking for you? Are you lost?" He slapped his suspenders and guffawed.

I tipped my head, careening around D who blocked my line of sight to the carnival. Maybe they were there. Having fun without me, hoping I'd answer the call of cotton candy's sugary goodness. "I guess you could say that."

"Tell me about these friends," he said with an eager curiosity.

I scratched my head. "Well one is short and gothic. The other is blonde and pretty."

His eyes grew big and got this strange light to them. "Blonde you say?"

I nodded. "Her name is Cindy."

Mr. D. choked. "And this, er...Cindy, you say? Did she wear a blue sparkly barrette?" He cleared his throat and coughed into his gloved hand.

"Yes!" My pulse quickened.

"And her friend? She's goth?" He rocked on his heels, slapping the suspenders against his fat chest.

"Yes. Goth." My brow furrowed without my permission. How did he not know what goth was? "They dress in dark colors like they're going to a funeral."

Mr. D. choked again. "Does the goth one wear a red cloak and have black hair?"

My smile broadened. He knew them! "Yes! And a fedora!" But suddenly the smile faded as my necklace strobed brighter and brighter. I realized something horrible. This guy had to be a creeper. No one could possibly have this information without collecting data first. "Wait. How'd you know all that?"

He giggled with a tee-hee sound.

"Have you seen them?"

"Nope!" he laughed again.

"But you just said..."

"But nothing." he cackled. "Nothing but reflections."

"Reflections?" My heart thudded. I'd heard that phrase from Hunter. And the crazy man at the movies had said the same exact thing. This clown was obviously insane. If the light coming from my necklace truly was a warning, I definitely needed to get away fast!

BRAIN FREEZE

Steve: Don't just stand there. ¡Vámonos!

"Riiiiiight." I backed away slowly. One foot behind the other. Obeying the necklace's—and my gut's—warning. "Well, um, thanks for your...help." I plastered a fake smile on my face. There's no way I could let on that I was nervous. Creepy stalkers were unpredictable. "So nice meeting you. I'm on my way now."

His hand shot out and grabbed my shoulder. "Where do you think you're going?" His voice came as a stern, low growl. It was a sudden change from the giggles he'd been producing.

His eyes narrowed into thin black slits. "No one leaves the Underworld!"

I gulped. "U-u-underworld?" I didn't need to be a local to figure out what that meant.

"Where else?" he said.

"You mean where dead people go?"

"Of course!" he nodded and gave a small, welcoming bow.

"Oh no, there must be some mistake, you see, I'm not dead."

Mr. D. cackled in disbelief.

"I fell through a mirror!" Oh great. Now I sounded just as crazy as the old clown.

"A mirror, you say?"

"Yes!" I agreed enthusiastically.

"That's not possible, Dearie!" He seemed to grow angry, gritting his teeth. But it was only temporary because he laughed again. What was it with this man and his laughing? "There's only one portal to the Underworld!" He smiled wickedly. "And that's through the grave!"

Chapter 22

"GRAVE? I don't even have a grave!" I protested.

"Nonsense!" He laughed, linking my elbow with his. Then he skipped along the path, my body lurching to the right then left as he towed me like a broken-down car.

We reached a striped booth. "Hello there, Bert!" chirped the clown.

A guy manning the station groaned. A Yankee's cap sat atop his head. He lit a cigar and placed it between his teeth as he leaned forward.

I shrieked. A corpse! Bert's skin was missing in patches and an eyeball dangled from its socket. My head felt dizzy and I struggled to stand.

"Hello, Mr. Death," Bert said, puffing his cigar.

"Mr. Death!" I gasped. "You mean…you're the…"

"The one and only!" Mr. Death bowed, sweeping his top hat across his body in a formal fashion, making a big show of it all.

My necklace didn't need to warn me again because the thudding of my heart did. "Oohhh…" I said. It came across as a gasp and a howl. "I knew there was more to your name than just D."

He laughed so hard his belly shook. "You got me!

Pardon me for teasing you before. I suppose we haven't been properly introduced!" He took a step back and flourished his top hat. "Mr. Death, Underworld Caretaker at your service!" He tossed his hat into the air. As it tumbled from the sky, he tipped his head and the hat landed gracefully, settling perfectly between his ears and meeting his brow. "And you are?"

"Sarah White." A shy smile crept onto my face. He might have been a clown, and he might have been the caretaker of the Underworld, but he seemed friendly enough. Besides, if he couldn't help me, I was sure no one could. And I started to feel comfortable in a strange sort of way, despite the fact that I was in a world filled with the dead. Maybe that's the only reason my necklace was going crazy.

"Lovely to meet you!" He sprang up onto his toes and shook my hand with so much enthusiasm it almost qualified as an act of violence. He turned his attention back to the ticket booth. "So, Bert, if you will. One ticket for my R.D., Sarah here, please!"

"R.D.?" I twiddled with my necklace.

"Well of course." Mr. Death rocked on his heels. "That's an abbreviation for Recently Deceased."

"B...b...but I told you, I'm not dead." My knees knocked.

Bert sighed loudly, a puff of smoke drifting from his cigar. "Oonnne ticket coooming up." He picked up a slip of paper and handed it to Mr. Death. "Thank youuu. Coommme agaiiian. Hv-a-nc-dy." Bert twirled the cigar in his mouth.

Mr. Death read the ticket, checking the information

with the tip of his gloved finger, before handing it to me. "Here you are, Dearie!"

"What's this for?" I smoothed the paper between my fingers.

"Read it! It should explain everything." Mr. Death twisted and contorted. The buttons popped off his shirt. The buckle burst off his suspenders and nearly hit me in the eye. His hat leapt off his head. Mr. Death shrunk down to the size of a marble. All that lay on the ground was a pile of clothes that looked like an ice cream sundae. The hat a perfect black cherry on top.

"Well that was odd," I said staring at the mound of fabric.

The tip of Bert's cigar burned a steady red. "Ummmmm hummmm," Bert buzzed through his half-decayed lips.

I was guessing he'd seen the disappearing act before. The pile of clothes moved before my very eyes and a small beetle scuttled out and tapped my foot. It raised its horny claw-like hand, then flew off.

I shivered. "Creepy."

Creepy: You callllllled?

Rubbing my head, I flipped the ticket over in my hands. The top side read:

Admission
One-way ticket to the Underworld

On the backside it had the most curious of all information.

Microscopic print said:

**All questions may be answered by the Undertaker.
No returns. All sales are final. Keep away from the
Dark Forest and enjoy your stay.**

The Dark Forest? That must have been where I came from. Enjoy my stay? Well, it's not like I could go anywhere else! I hadn't figured a way out and everyone thought I was deceased. As if! I was alive and well. Beating heart and all.

I turned to Bert who was flipping through a magazine.

"Can you tell me where to find house number...?" I glanced down at the ticket in my hand. "Number 664?"

BRAIN FREEZE

Creepy: It should be six six siiiiixxxxx.
Crawly: Oh yes. Triple six for sure.
Steve: Would you two please behave?
Icky: Isn't that...the Master's number?
Yucky: We like the Master.
Steve: Zip it!

Bert didn't respond. He just sat there and continued turning the pages.

"Excuse me. Bert?"

He turned his back to me and grumbled.

I had never been so insulted in all my life. "The Dead are so rude. I'll just find it myself." I huffed.

Bert swung back around, his eyeball swinging like a pendulum. "Youuuuu saaaaay the Dead are ruuuuuuude?'

I nodded.

"So, you reaaaaaaally are one of the Living?"

I nodded again. "I know Mr. Death is convinced I died when I fell through that mirror. But I survived." I held out my wrist so Bert could feel my pulse. "See?"

Bert leaned back and took a long draw from his cigar,

the tip burning a bright red. He sat there motionless staring like I was some sort of freak.

"Fine." I threw my hands into the air. Talking to the dead was like talking to...I don't know! But it was a real pain in the butt. "I'll find it myself." A cobblestone path led me away from the Ferris wheel and as the carnival disappeared into the horizon, the smells faded, too. I was going to find my house. Then I was going to figure out a way to get the heck out of here.

Chapter 23

A girl on a mission, I marched along the path. Turquoise meadows with pink daises sprung up along the path. An iridescent green moth fluttered onto my nose and I sneezed. He drifted away and I quickly lent my finger as a landing pad. From out of nowhere, a bird swooped down and ate him. "That wasn't very nice."

"Caw!" the crow called.

"And you're not a very nice old bird." I couldn't believe he'd eaten a perfectly lovely moth. Plus, he could have taken my finger with it!

"Koww!" he crowed.

"Is that all you can say? Wait." I waved my hand at him so he wouldn't respond. "Don't answer that."

"Scream!" The bird settled on a branch.

"I kneeeew it." I threw my hands up in the air. "What do you want from me anyway?" I strode past the tree he'd settled in and kept my eyes forward, intent on finding my house.

The bird glided ahead and landed in a tree. "CAW!" His beak clacked as he snapped it shut.

"What's wrong with you? Freak." This bird obviously had issues. Just like everything around here. Rude Bert who refused to speak to me. Mr. Death who shifted into a beetle. A Dark Forest that tortured me. A field full of eyeballs. And oh yeah, a strange creature in a tunnel that would have eaten me alive if it hadn't been for a talking skeleton mouse that sacrificed his life for mine.

"Raven freak!" The bird flapped his wings franticly as he bobbed his head up and down. "Raven!"

"Yes. You're a freak!" I kicked a pebble and it skittered across the path. "But you're not a raven. You're a crow."

"Raven!"

"You're clearly a crow. You're not a raven." I paused, wondering about this strange bird. What was he doing anyway? I'd never seen a bird behave in such a manner. "Sounds like a personal problem."

"Raven! Raven! Raven!" The crow bobbed his head.

"You're trying to tell me something, aren't you?"

The bird danced excitedly on the branch.

"Two caws for yes?" I squinted. "One for no?"

"Caw, caw!"

"Okay. Well…let me guess." I tapped my chin, thinking. "A Raven is a type of bird?"

"Koww!" he crowed, shaking his head.

"Not a bird? Hmmm…" I said.

"Raven." The bird used his wing as a finger and tapped the tip of his feather against his chest. "Raven."

"Oh my!" How could I have been so stupid? "Raven. It's your name! You're a crow named Raven!"

"Caw, caw!" He soared into the sky and then nosedived back down bullet fast. He banked left at the last second and swooped up, landing on the branch over my head.

I felt bad for calling him stupid in the forest. "You're a very smart bird, aren't you?"

"Caw, caw!" he said beating his chest with a single wing.

"Of course, you are." I smiled with relief, knowing that, for the first time in hours—a day? How long had I been here, anyway?—I'd made a friend. "Well, I do believe it's time to move forward, Mr. Raven. I really need to find house number 664."

"Caw, caw!" He flapped ahead, urging me to follow him. Keeping pace with Raven, content that he would lead the way and take me to my new little house in the Underworld, there was nearly a spring in my step.

"Raven?" I asked. "Do you think I can get out of here?"

He peered over his shoulder and his sad eyes gave me the answer. As much as I didn't want it to be true, I knew it was.

"But there's got to be a way out." The tears pricked at my eyes.

"Caw, caw," he crowed, as if he just realized something. Raven waved a wing before banking right.

I double-stepped to catch up to him. As soon as I did, he slowed, and I panted, completely out of breath. We'd made so many turns that the carnival was off to my right. But it was so far in the distance it barely looked like a blip in the horizon.

A field separated us, the grasses waist-high, filled with tall sunflowers. Getting a closer look, I realized this plant wasn't anything I was familiar with.

My breath fell on the stalks, each exhale making the flower sway back and forth. The seed bulb at the end of the stalk opened. An eyeball! It blinked twice and turned away.

"It's alive!" I should have known. Nothing in this world was at it seemed. Maybe these tall plants were the mothers and the little eyeballs in the grass were the seedlings. Either way, I wasn't interested in learning more. I needed to get out of here. But I was so disoriented, I didn't know which direction to run. I turned one way and saw another eyeball seed pod open. I screamed at it then punched its face. Darting left, another opened, and I did the same. Dozens of pods bobbed in the breeze, their freaky eyeball-blinking making the hairs on my arms stand on end.

I stopped to catch my breath and a hand squeezed my shoulder.

Chapter 24

"Relax. It's okay," said a sweet voice behind me. "These are just the All-Seeing Fields."

I gulped, staring straight ahead, the person still at my back. "What do they do?" When I tried to turn around, the hand gripped my shoulder tighter and I froze.

"Well, they *see things in the Underworld*," she said, her voice remaining kind and patient.

"What could they possibly need to see here? Everything is dead."

"Mr. Death keeps watch. He says it'll protect us from the evil spirits." The woman's tone changed as she whispered in my ear. "But the fields are not to be trusted." What she didn't say, but I heard was, "Neither is Mr. Death."

My necklace wasn't flashing a warning, so it seemed I could trust this woman. "I understand," I said with a nod.

"What's your name? Maybe I can find a relative you can stay with until..."

"A relative?" Good idea! I swirled around, breaking free from the grasp on my shoulder. When I saw the person I'd been talking to, it took a second for it to register. "Mrs. Stiltskin?" My knees went wobbly, like I'd been at sea for too long, and they buckled beneath me.

"Whoa, whoa, whoa." She grabbed my arm to stop my fall. "Are you all right?'

I nodded, but truth be told, I wasn't sure. My best friend's mother who died a few months ago was in the Underworld with me. It all felt too strange and I didn't like it. I just wanted out of this creepy place.

"How did you know my name?" The woman helped me to my feet.

"Don't you recognize me? It's Sarah," I said, backing away so there was some distance between us. While I waited for her to say something, I volunteered, "And I have a dead aunt on my father's side. Just in case—"

"Sarah?" A sharp line formed between her eyebrows as her voice grew weak. The woman swallowed hard and her face blanched. "Sarah White is that really you?" We stared at each other in silence. Then she knelt down with her arms outstretched as a tear ran down her cheek.

I ran as fast as the tears streaming down my cheeks and leapt into her arms. She squeezed me tight. My chest heaved so hard that a strange sounding musical sob exploded out. B flat, for sure. Maybe an A sharp.

All this time, I thought I was lost and alone. Finally, a familiar face. Cindy's mom was the nicest lady I'd ever known.

"What are you doing here?" She broke the embrace and held me at arms' length. I didn't need to tell her why I was here. She must have had an idea. There was only one reason anyone came to the Underworld.

"I'm not sure. One minute everything was fine and the next I was here. I just don't know."

Something crossed her face, causing her eyebrows to furrow. "Never mind that."

"Tell me about the evil spirits. Who are they?" Raven swooped down and landed on my shoulder, his claws digging into my skin. "More important....Ouch." I grunted and Raven loosened his grip. He followed it with a soft, apologetic caw. "*Where* are they?"

"The spirits? They're the ones who live in the Dark Forest over there." She gestured towards the woods that I'd passed through. The ones that had delivered me into the Underworld.

"I just came from that way. No one lives over there."

She gasped so hard she coughed. "You *what?*"

"Those dark trees. I came from there." I tipped my head towards the woods. "That's how I found him." I petted Raven on the head, and he pressed against my palm.

"But that's not possible." Mrs. Stiltskin took a single step backward. "You're not evil. Are you?" She raised an eyebrow as she chuckled.

"Of course not!" But I paused because after all I'd been through, I felt like I couldn't be too sure about anything anymore. "At least I don't *feel* evil. Do I *look* evil?" I hadn't seen myself in hours—or was it days? It felt impossible to know how much time had passed.

Her expression softened as she put a finger to her lips. "No. You look like the same Sarah White I remember. With the exception of all those cuts and bruises."

"Well, that's a relief."

She looked past me, shaking her head. "How did you end up over there?"

"It was my birthday. We were celebrating and playing a game of laser tag. Things got a little out of hand and I fell through a mirror."

"How on earth did you do that?"

"I'm not sure. But I can tell you that I didn't die." If the stinging cuts on my arms were any indication of my mortality, then I was confident death hadn't come upon me just yet. "My family and friends saw the whole thing. When I was on the other side of the mirror, I could see them, but they couldn't see me. They were really upset. They told me they'd come find me and I should stay put. But then I couldn't because there was something in the cave."

"What cave?" Mrs. Stiltskin questioned.

How come she didn't know about the cave? "The one in the hillside at the end of the Dark Forest. Something in there wanted to eat me. At least that's what it seemed like anyway. It definitely wasn't playing tag."

"But the cave is where...." Mrs. Stiltskin trailed off as she slowly pressed her lips into a thin line. She was definitely avoiding telling me any further information. I had a feeling that was a smart move. Whatever was in that cave was probably more dangerous than I cared to know. "Tell me more about the mirror."

"My mom thought maybe it was from her cousin Phillip, but the carvings weren't his work."

"What kind of carvings?"

"A forest of trees. Really creepy leafless branches with birds crouched on the limbs. Now that I've been through the Dark Forest, I see the similarity. It's a bit eerie, you know? Like someone wanted me to be sucked into that mirror and see the forest for myself."

"A portal," Mrs. Stiltskin said with a gasp. "There's only one person who is capable of that."

Chapter 25

"A portal?" I gasped.

Mrs. Stiltskin grabbed my arm. "Come inside. Quickly, quickly."

Raven flapped his wings, digging his claws into my shoulder before flying off and landing on the roof of the cottage. He crowed loudly as Mrs. Stiltskin swiftly closed the door behind us.

"Sit." She pointed at a stool at the kitchen counter.

My mouth was as dry as a cracker. "Water. Pu...please."

"I'm so sorry. You must be so confused and scared." She pulled her stool up next to mine and sat down. "It's a lot to take in and I'm not making that any easier. Am I?"

I shook my head. "It's okay."

She gazed into my eyes and then snapped back, leaping off her stool. "Water. You wanted a glass of water." Mrs. Stiltskin retrieved a yellow pitcher from the fridge. Her hand trembled as she filled two glasses, water splashing onto the counter. She gulped down her drink. "Tell me everything. The whole story. Including your arrival in the Underworld."

I fiddled with my hands as I recounted the events that lead me here. "Well, I received the mirror for my birthday. Like I mentioned earlier, my mom thought it was from her brother, but it wasn't. We never did figure out who sent it."

"Anonymous?" Mrs. Stiltskin sat back down and then neatly folded her hands in her lap.

"Yeah. I guess so."

Mrs. Stiltskin twiddled her thumbs. "This is all very strange."

"I know, right? That's what I thought!"

"Unless..." She paused. "Well, we can't worry about that now."

"Wait a minute. You said there was only one person who was capable of creating a portal. You know who did this, don't you? Because if you know, then maybe they can help me get back!" My thoughts drifted to all I'd been through and my body shook violently.

"Sarah, it's going to be okay." She patted my knee. "We're going to get you out of here."

I took a few deep breaths as I stared down at my hands. When I glanced up, I noticed a far-off look in Mrs. Stiltskin's eyes. "You know, Cindy was at the party, too." I smiled, hoping it would make her feel better. "She lost the game early on and left right at dusk. Seemed like she was in a hurry."

"Cindy," she whispered, turning away. "How is my girl?" Her voice got a little warble in it and I didn't need to see her face to know that she was crying.

I put my hand on her arm. "She misses you. Still, she's learned to be happy." I pulled away, tucking a strand of hair behind my ear. "But she stinks at laser tag."

Mrs. Stiltskin burst out laughing. She reached for a tissue and wiped away her tears as she smiled.

"I'll tell her I saw you—"

She dropped her napkin on the counter as if something very important had dawned on her. "You said Cindy left in a hurry? What time was that?"

"It was dusk. So maybe around six thirty or so."

Mrs. Stiltskin sat there, staring at me. Staring *through* me. "When were you transported here?" She grabbed my shoulders and gave a little shake as she stared into my eyes. "Think hard. Think very, very hard." "

"It was dark outside when I fell through the mirror. Yes. It was definitely dark."

"Are you sure?"

"I'm positive. After Cindy left, Hunter and I continued the game of laser tag. I fell through the mirror and I've been here ever since." I shrugged. "Which is pretty much forever. Or, at least it feels that way. I guess it could just be a few hours."

"Have you seen a sunset?" She paused. "Or I suppose I mean a sunrise."

"Uh…I'm not sure."

"This is important." Mrs. Stiltskin's face screwed up as she leaned closer.

Her earnest efforts made my head hurt. Time seemed so different here and I just couldn't grasp how much had passed. "I'm sorry. I don't know. I just don't know."

Mrs. Stiltskin leaned back. "Never mind." She swallowed hard and then took a slow, steady breath. "Just finish telling your story. What happened next?"

"That's when my sister and I had a stand-off. And before I'd even gone to my room it had grown dark because I even remembered thinking to myself that I needed a flashlight. When I'd gone to my room it was almost black outside. And…" I almost mentioned the glowing necklace and how it was easy to see in the dark room. But I stopped myself.

"And what, Sarah? This is important."

"And then… I fell through the mirror." The dark empty hole where I fell endlessly before landing in the tunnel. The mirror that brought me to a strange place with a creature that wanted to eat me, a crow named Raven, and an Underworld Carnival. The mirror that had me trapped in a place where I would never see my thirteenth birthday.

"You know what?" she asked.

"What?" I asked out of a knee-jerk response because I was too dazed to really think about anything at this point.

She danced from foot to foot as she gasped out her

words. "I didn't think there was anything we could do. But..."

I snapped out of my daze. "But...but WHAT?"

"I think I can help you before—"

"You can help me?" I was too excited to let her finish her sentence. I really liked the sound of those words. They were music to my ears. And not creepy Underworld carnival music. "What's your plan?"

"We're going to get you home."

Home. What a wonderful little word. Filled with promise and loved ones and family. "Yes please!" My body tingled with hopeful anticipation.

"I'll have to make a few arrangements with Cheddar."

I leapt to my feet. "You know Cheddar?"

"Of course." Mrs. Stiltskin laughed. "He was Cindy's..." She stopped mid-sentence.

"Her pet?" I raised an eyebrow.

"Yes, you could say that."

There was an awkward pause. Cheddar had sacrificed himself so I could escape. There was no easy way to tell her this. I opted for the direct approach. "Cheddar is dead."

Chapter 26

She nodded with a chuckle. "Of course he is. That's why he's in the Underworld."

"No, I mean, he's really dead. Cheddar attacked the creature that wanted to eat me so I could escape. He sacrificed himself for me."

Mrs. Stiltskin patted her chest over her heart as she laughed. "Oh honey. You can't harm anything in the Underworld. It's already dead."

"You...you can't?" My skin prickled with embarrassment. "So, what happened to him then?"

"I'll tell you what happened to me." Cheddar scampered out from behind a basket on the counter. "After I saved your sorry butt, I had to reassemble my bones." He raised his fist and shook it. "Do you know how difficult that is? There's over two hundred of these suckers. It's like a puzzle. I hate puzzles!"

"Now, now Cheddar." Mrs. Stiltskin patted him on the head. "Don't get yourself all worked up. You know what happens when you do."

Cheddar folded his arms and humpfed. "Fine. But see if I'll do another favor for this one ever again." He thumbed his would-be nose at me.

"It was a very kind thing you did," she said. "So kind, in

fact, you deserve a special reward." She opened the fridge and pulled out a plate of various cheeses and placed it on the counter next to him. "For my good boy."

Cheddar squeaked, grabbed a piece of cheese, and scampered off into a hole in the wall.

I swiped a slice from the plate and took a bite. "It's a good thing Cindy never witnessed him talking. He might not be one of her favorite pets anymore if she heard how cranky he was."

Mrs. Stiltskin laughed uncomfortably as she shifted from foot to foot.

"I'm hysterical." I laughed along with her, thinking that death had made Mrs. Stiltskin loose her marbles. But why did it feel like I was about to lose mine?

"Now what were we talking about?" She cleared her throat.

"Home," I said, threading my fingers together, each of them feeling terribly cold with a weird frost-bite sensation. My pinky finger wobbled. It cracked away from my hand and fell off. My eyes grew huge as I looked at my finger lying on the floor. "What in the...?" I sucked in a fast breath. *More hallucinations. It had to be.*

"Did you say something?"

"Uhhh..." I hesitated, still staring at the finger on the floor. "Uh, you were going to find a way to get me home."

"Ah yes. Let's see...." She rummaged through her kitchen drawers, talking to herself.

Just as I suspected. She'd lost her marbles. My eyes darted to my hand, looking at the empty space where my pinky had once been. I wiggled my fingers. The digit on the floor danced like a worm. Snatching it up, I quickly shoved it back on my hand.

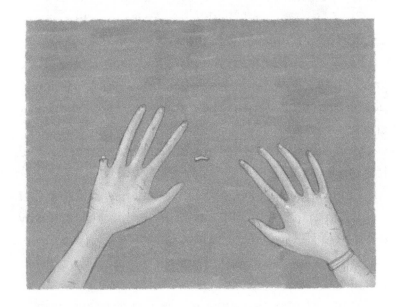

"It has to be before sunset of the second day." She lifted a suspicious looking spoon and held it mid-air. "And, of course, there's the threat of Mr. Death."

"Mr. Death? Uuumm...what are you talking about?" I squirmed in my seat, but my butt felt numb just like my finger. Oh no! Was I about to discover what it would feel like when Mom said she 'worked her butt off'? I blinked bringing my attention back to the conversation.

"Mr. Death," Mrs. Stiltskin repeated, staring at the spoon she was holding. "He's a..."

"A tad creepy but he's super friendly. Like you said, he uses the All-Seeing Fields to protect us from the evil spirits in the Dark Forest. So, he can't be so bad, can he?"

She blinked, lowering the spoon and plastering a fake smile on her face. I knew it was fake because of the way her eyes lost their sparkle. "Look, there's some things that are better off hidden."

She was right. That's why it was best she didn't know I was losing pieces of myself. I tucked my hands behind my back.

But maybe there was something not quite right about Mr. Death. My necklace did light up when he was near. If Cheddar was right, then the charm was definitely warning me about Mr. Death.

"It's going to be a while before I can get you out of here. But I'm sure I can do it before the next sunset. And if my calculations are correct." She counted on her fingers, her lips moving but her voice silent. "Then I'll have just enough time and you'll…"

"I'll…?"

"You'll be fine. Perfectly fine." She straightened her dress, smoothing out the wrinkles. "I have to organize a few things first. Which means you'll need to be patient. You can do that, right? Be patient, I mean."

I nodded, my legs feeling like I'd been forced to run laps in gym. "If it means getting out of here, I can wait." I stared at my reattached finger and wondered how long it would hold. Maybe I needed to escape this place faster than both of us realized. It may even already be too late.

"Great. In the meantime, why don't you get some sleep? You can stay in Cindy's….I mean the guest room." She still expected to see her daughter again. How sad. And a little bit morbid. She opened a door to a cute bedroom that suited Cindy's tastes perfectly. As I reached for the handle, she gasped. "Goodness! How did I over-look that?"

My pinky! Oh no. "What?" My hand shook.

"You! Look at you. You're filthy," she said as she surveyed me. "And covered in cuts and bruises." She bustled across the room and opened a small closet. "I bet you'd give anything for a nice hot bath."

I nodded. She wasn't even my mother and she still seemed to know exactly what I needed.

Mrs. Stiltskin pulled fresh towels from the closet and placed them on the bed. Their April-freshness floated straight to my nostrils and I breathed it in deep. It made my chest ache as the fragrance reminded me of home.

"Thanks. That sounds perfect right about now." I grabbed the towel and hugged it to my chest. "You're so kind. I'm sorry that—"

"Make yourself comfortable." Mrs. Stiltskin swooped me into her arms, embracing me in a tight hug.

"I will," I said. "And thank you."

Mrs. Stiltskin reached for a cloak which hung from a hook near the door. "I'm heading out to look into getting you out of here. I'll only be a few minutes. There's some spare clothes in the drawer. I think you and Cindy are about the same size." She pointed at a mirrored dresser before slipping her arms in the sleeves of the coat.

Wow. She really did expect to see her daughter. My throat choked up thinking about my best friend in the Underworld. I'd hate to lose her. I couldn't think of anything that would be worse than losing my best friend. Except, of course, losing my mom. Good thing neither of those were going to happen. At least not anytime soon.

"Bathroom is that way." She pointed to a small hallway on the other side of the kitchen.

"Thank you, Mrs. Stiltskin." When she left the room, I waited for the sound of the front door clicking shut before I rummaged through the dresser. The first drawer contained socks and pajamas. What I really needed were a pair of jeans and a t-shirt to replace the battered ones clinging to my body. And there they were, right in the second drawer!

The front door creaked open. "Whatever you do, don't leave this house!" Mrs. Stiltskin called.

"I won't."

"Promise me." She held her fingers in the air like a pledge.

Going back out into the Underworld by myself wasn't exactly my idea of fun. "I promise." I made an 'x' over my heart, hoping my index finger wouldn't fall off. "I swear."

"Good. Now go enjoy your bath." She started to pull the door shut, then turned back. "And get some rest."

I saluted like a soldier. "Got it."

As soon as she left, I slipped into a nice, warm bath with lots of bubbles. After a good long soak, I found some bandages in the medicine cabinet and placed them on my worst cuts. I also wrapped that pinky finger on tight. That sucker wasn't falling off again if I had any control over it! Slipping my birthday bracelet from Cindy back on my wrist, I smiled. She'd be so happy to know that I was with her mom. I dressed into the clean clothes which fit pretty well, though the pants were a tad short. Then I emptied the pockets of my old, dirty jeans and stuffed everything into the new pair. With a towel on my head, I walked back to the bedroom and curled up on the comfy mattress, realizing just how wonderful it felt against my tired, aching body.

A purring sound startled me, and I nearly leapt off the bed when I saw a skeleton cat crawl out from behind the pillow.

"A cat!" I yelped. "A skeleton cat!"

The cat crept toward me. He rubbed his head into my leg, purring violently.

"Wait…" I seemed to remember that Cindy mentioned she had a pet cat once. What was his name? Scrapper? Scrinchy? No, that wasn't right. Scruffy. Scruffy! That was it! "Good cat, Scruffy." I scrubbed my fingertips over his skull while he purred peacefully, and I drifted off to sleep.

Hours later, I awoke to someone shaking my shoulder.

Chapter 27

"Ten more minutes, Mom." My eyes struggled to open. They fluttered but my vision remained fuzzy.

"I'm not your mother, Honey, but I'm sure she'd love to see you."

I sat up in a start and rubbed my eyes.

"That's why we've got to get you out of here," Mrs. Stiltskin said.

I glanced around the room at the blue painted walls, the soft bed, and the bookshelves around the window to the backyard. A backyard that didn't look like anything that I'd ever seen before. "Where am I?"

"My cottage in the Underworld." Mrs. Stiltskin sat on the edge of the bed. "Remember?"

The sudden smell of cotton candy drifted through the window. "Yes. I remember now." Shuffling out of bed, I noticed a piece of rotting flesh on my foot. Cheese and rice! What was happening to me? I quickly pulled on a pair of socks before Mrs. Stiltskin had a chance to see it.

"I have some food ready. Come eat." Mrs. Stiltskin bustled into the kitchen and I followed close behind.

Another smell tickled my nostrils and I lifted my nose to the ceiling, inhaling deeply. Something smelled super yummy. Like smarts. Book smarts. I scratched my scalp and a clump of my gorgeous curls, still attached to a piece of skin, fell to the floor. My eyes felt like they would pop out of my head. My beautiful hair! I was literally falling to pieces! I sucked in a deep breath trying to calm myself.

"What did you make?" My stomach growled with a very strange craving for protein. One of my mom's omelets would be perfect right about now. She always said she could make a mean one although I'm not sure how it was mean. It never said anything bad to me.

"Oh, just fried brains. Think of them like scrambled eggs." She dumped half of the mixture and it slowly slopped out of the pan and onto a plate. Plop. Plop. Slurp. Mrs. Stiltskin slid it in front of me and I crinkled my nose in disgust.

BRAIN FREEZE

Creepy: Braaaaaiiiinsssss.
*Stinky: That would go great with my drink. *burps**
Yucky: Heh-heh. Just make sure they're warm.

The voices hadn't made an appearance in quite a while. In some odd way, I realized how I'd missed them. Almost. Plus, they sure seemed to have an appetite for the strangest things.

"What's the matter? Don't you like them?" She licked a spoon. "They were the brains of a scholar once. He was very....oh, what's the phrase?" Her face lit up as she raised the spoon in the air. "Ah! Book smart!"

"A scholar?" I choked.

"That's what the man at the food stand said. Fresh and real, gua-ran-teed!" Mrs. Stiltskin tapped the spoon on the counter. "No phony dumb brains in this house!"

My stomach revolted. "You're kidding."

"What? Do they smell fake?" she asked, studying the package. "Undercooked perhaps?" She lifted the pan and stirred the mixture at eye level.

"Umm no." Confused at this entire exchange, I scratched my head and felt the missing flesh of my scalp. I mean, who ate brains? "How would I be able to smell a fake brain anyway?"

"Well, it smells stupid." Mrs. Stiltskin said this plainly, as if it were the obvious explanation.

I wasn't sure what stupid smelled like, but I didn't say anything more.

"Now eat up, okay? You'll need your strength. Besides," She grabbed a bag off the hook by the door and said, "It's not like I haven't noticed you're falling to pieces. First a finger, then your hair. Never know what's coming next." She smiled before adding, "The food will do the trick. Trust me. Eat up. I'll be back soon. I've got some more work to do." She exited through the front door then turned back. "Oh, and remember, whatever you do, don't leave this house."

"Got it." As soon as she closed the door behind her I poked my fork into the glop. The gelatinous mixture wiggled in response. I stabbed my fork all the way into the center of the grayish matter and brought it to my mouth.

It didn't *smell* terrible. I wondered if it would *taste* okay. Quickly, I shoved the bite in. Slimy, mushy, salty sludge. Gross! I swallowed the mouthful only because I hoped Mrs. Stiltskin was right. Maybe I'd stop falling to pieces. But one bite should be enough, right? I didn't have to eat the entire thing, did I? Lifting my plate, I carried it to the trash can.

Creepy: Well, if you're not going to eat iiiiiiiit, give some to ussssssss!

I was almost relieved to hear another voice again. How strange to think, hearing them actually made me feel normal.

Slimy: Aren't you going to give it to us? We're starving in here.

"Yeah, yeah, I hear you," I said, ignoring the way my head spun like a dreidel. "And I know I'm not crazy." This was nothing compared to half the stuff in the Underworld. "What are you, anyway? I know *who* you are. Since I can't see you, you owe it to me to at least tell me *what* you are."

BRAIN FREEZE

Steve: Well, we're . . . worms.
Several voices humphed in unison.
Crawly: And we happen to be living inside your head. Heh-heh.
Stinky: Which, if you ask us, is quite small.
Yucky: And lacking food!
Creepy: Now feed us those braaaaiiiiinssssss.

You mean to tell me these voices weren't just my thoughts? There are actually real, live worms living in my head?! EWWWW! EWWWW! I dropped the plate on the counter and batted my hands on either side of my skull. "Get out! Get out! Get out!!"

Creepy: Ssssssimmer down noooow!
Steve: You're loud enough to wake the undead, Miss Sarah.
Slimy: You might lose your head.

They were right. If my finger fell off so easily, I might decapitate myself just by hitting my skull! Suddenly realizing the insults they'd slung at me, I shouted, "Hey, wait a minute. My brain's not small!"

BRAIN FREEZE

Icky: You're one to talk. *sneezes* You're not crammed in here with four other worms!
Yucky: Including one that keeps spreading his germs.
Steve: Yes. We've been over this already. But you're wrong. There's seven of us. Can't you count, Icky?
Creepy: Try to keep up, pleasssse.
Slimy: We don't like repeating ourselves.

"Seven. Worms." I stumbled around feeling uneasy. I could almost have dealt with seven voices when I believed it was merely my own thoughts. But worms? That was another thing altogether. "Seven!"

BRAIN FREEZE

Stinky: You can count. *slow claps* Good for you.

"Duh. Of course I can count." I crossed my arms with a huff. But a tearing sound at my shoulder stopped me. I couldn't lose a limb! "Now can you please explain what you're doing in my head?"

BRAIN FREEZE

Steve: We're your worms!

"Yes. You said that already." I rubbed at my shoulder. "By the way. That. Is. So. Gross."

BRAIN FREEZE

Steve: We're not gross. Well, Slimy is. Oh, and in case you need a reminder, my name's Steve.

Unbelievable. "Steve?"

BRAIN FREEZE

Steve: Probably best if you warm up to us. We're a permanent fixture here.

"Wait. What? You mean this is permanent?" I took my plate and started for the trash can again. They were suddenly quiet, obviously avoiding an answer. "Stupid worms," I muttered as I studied the plate of brains. Should I really feed them? What if it made things worse? I couldn't stand the thought of them bothering me much more. I stared at my bandaged finger. But what if it made me better?

There was no choice. I gulped down another mouthful because I didn't want to lose any more pieces of myself. Not even a single strand of hair. Especially if it was attached to a chunk of my scalp.

Surprisingly, my taste buds shouted in triumph. Saliva dribbled down my chin and I shoveled another bite into my mouth. Then another. And another. I ate until the entire serving was gone and I longed for more. Then I licked the plate clean. Hoping no one saw my uncivilized behavior, I quickly dapped my mouth with a napkin. That's when I noticed the strange color of the sky. Although it was once lavender, it had changed to a sickly orange-yellow. Even though Cindy's mom told me not to leave, I had to figure out why the sky had changed.

If this had anything to do with evil spirits, then I wanted out of the Underworld as fast as possible! Those eyes in the field might be able to help me. Since they're all-seeing, as Mrs. Stiltskin had said, then they'd know if evil spirits were lurking around. I slipped out the door. "I just won't go too far," I whispered to myself.

As soon as I stepped outside, Raven swooped down, landing on my shoulder, like he'd been waiting for me all that time.

It felt colder than before, and I rubbed my arms, wishing I'd grabbed a sweater. The sky threatened a storm, but what did I know? It could just be like that this time of day. After all, I only arrived a few hours ago. Or was it a day?

I couldn't remember and my head hurt from thinking so hard. Or maybe that was the worms squirming around in there.

With determination, I retraced my steps back to the All-Seeing Fields. The grass swayed in the wind, the seed pods bouncing in response. One blinked opened. Then, the rest of the pods opened in a wave. The eyes on the ground fluttered open, too.

Raven cawed. He seemed uneasy as he tightened his grip on my shoulder. With the way my body was falling to pieces, I hoped he wouldn't rip my arm off.

"Hello," I sang in a bird-like voice. "Hello, hello."

The pods blinked in response. I blinked back. The eyes widened as if somehow startled.

"Hmmmm…I wonder." I knelt down, putting my eyes level with the seed pods and staring straight into the cornea, I winked. They blinked once, very slowly. Then they started to blink like strobe lights. No. Like Morse code. Were they trying to tell me something? My necklace strobed, too. The blinking stopped suddenly. The eyes widened and snapped shut tighter than a padlock on a door. "What's wrong? Was it something I blinked?"

Steve: *Get outta there!*
Creepy: *Yeah, what are you waitiiiiing foooor?*
Stinky: *Move those legs, Missy.*

Yucky: Maybe you can help her Stinky. Use your gas as a jet propulsion.
Crawly: She's not Missy. Her name's Sarah.
Stinky: I know what her name is. *force farts*
Crawly: Then why'd you call—
Stinky: Never mind. Just get her legs walking or we're all fried!
Icky: No one likes fried worms. *achoo!*
Slimy: Not even big, fat, juicy ones?
Steve: No. Not even big, fat, juicy ones.
Slimy: How about eensie, weensy, squeensy ones?
Steve: Not even eensie, weensy, squeensy ones.
Slimy: Well, that's good news for me.
Steve: Enough already! Time to take control of the motherboard. We need to get out of here before we're toast.

I didn't know why, but I had the strangest sensation to run. Almost like someone—or something—was doing it for me. The worms had taken control. My legs moved and I headed straight back to Mrs. Stiltskin's cottage. As soon as it was in sight, Raven flew to the rooftop. The door slammed shut, helped by a gust of wind, and I leaned against it, panting.

"Were you talking again?" I asked my worms. "Because I could swear you said something."

Creepy: Nope. Not ussssss.
Yucky: Never. We wouldn't talk.

Crawly: And we'd never make you do things. Heh-heh.
Steve: Not unless—

"Unless what…" I asked as the door burst open behind me. In the doorway stood Mrs. Stiltskin. Her eyes glowed a sickly yellow and she marched across the threshold, heading straight at me.

Chapter 28

Mrs. Stiltskin slammed a rolled-up paper on the counter. In the light of the cottage, her eyes returned to their normal color.

My heart thudded in my chest. "Back so soon?"

"Yes, and apparently you've been here longer than we both thought." She held up the newspaper and unrolled it revealing a headline.

Beneath that was my mugshot, followed by one of that rat, Bert. Worse, the date on the newspaper read two whole days past my birthday party.

"I'm in the paper?" I gulped.

"Looks that way," said Mrs. Stiltskin. "If you want to make it out of here alive, you've got to hurry."

My throat tightened.

"And if you don't cooperate and do exactly what I tell you, then this," she said, her voice stern and frightening as she swept her hand across the room, "will be a very permanent, very bad reality."

"Permanent?" Just like my worms. I tried to swallow but my mouth was as dry as a cracker.

"Yes." She pulled me to my feet. "We need to move fast!"

My legs wobbled beneath me. Were they going to fall off? "I'm ready. Let's do this."

Mrs. Stiltskin flung the door open wide. A dark figure obscured the doorway. She gasped at the shadow. "Mr. Death. What are you doing here?" She stepped between us and pushed me back inside the house.

"You called?" he said with a cackle.

Although I still couldn't see him, I didn't need to, I recognized the voice immediately.

"There must be some mistake," Mrs. Stiltskin said.

Mr. Death pushed Cindy's mom aside. "I don't make mistakes." His shadow loomed over me.

My necklace began strobing. Danger. Just as Cheddar had warned me. "Called? You?" My brow furrowed displaying my confusion. I gulped and discreetly covered the charm with my hand. "Ummmm….no."

"Oh, I do believe so, Ms. Sarah White." He pushed past us, stepping into the cottage without permission. "You most certainly did." He bowed. But this wasn't a friendly bow with another formal introduction. No, it was one of those bows that screamed trouble. Mr. Death guffawed, a string of spit flying from his mouth.

"No. No, I didn't." I stepped back, bumping into the door.

"Why, of course you did. You woke my eyes."

I was in big trouble. "I didn't mean to."

"You were in the All-Seeing Fields?" Mrs. Stiltskin's voice raised sharply but her face showed concern.

Mr. Death slapped his suspenders in place. "They told me someone was here to see me!"

"Well...." I said, my voice wavering, "It was an accident. I didn't mean to wake them."

Mrs. Stiltskin frowned, and I knew I'd disappointed her. "You went out when I told you not to?" She looked away, lowering her head with a shake

"And that's what my eyes are there for!" Mr. Death had a jolly lilt to his voice that was a little too creepy. "They assist me."

"Well, we aren't in need of your assistance," Mrs. Stiltskin said, her voice stern as she gritted her teeth.

"Ah, but you see, I'm in need of yours." His voice echoed with a loud boom.

I backed away slowly. "Mine?"

He nodded and smiled menacingly. "But of course. Who else would I need? The Living don't leave the Underworld."

"I guess I should be on my way." Tiptoeing backward, I

slipped a hand into my pocket. Needed to look casual. Calm, cool, and collected. My fingers felt the corners of a small square of paper. My ticket! I pulled it out and held it up for all to see. "New death, new job. Places to go, undead to see."

"Of course, my dear! Wouldn't dream of you being late on your first day!" Mr. Death paused as he pulled at his suspenders. "In fact, why don't I escort you to your new job?"

That wasn't exactly the response I was looking for. "Oh, you don't have to do that. Really. It's fine." I waved my hands in protest. "I'm fine. Everything is fine."

"But I insist!" Mr. Death rocked on his heels before grabbing my arm.

"She's busy." Mrs. Stiltskin stepped forward, straightening her back. Even without her two-inch heels, she was taller than him.

"Why, of course she's busy. She has a job to do here." Mr. Death wasn't backing down and I could tell things were going to get ugly if I didn't cooperate.

I shoved the ticket back in my pocket. "It's okay. I'll go." This was a really vulnerable position I'd put myself in. What else could I do?

"But Sarah....you don't know—"

"It's fine. I wouldn't know my way there without his help." My nails dug into my palms as I curled my fingers into a fist. There was no telling what Mr. Death was capable of and I didn't want to find out. As much as I wanted to get out of the Underworld, this was the only way to protect Mrs. Stiltskin and myself.

"Well, just be back in time for dinner." Mrs. Stiltskin's

expression told me she was sorry she had just lost another child. First Cindy, and now me. And there was nothing she could do about it. She squeezed my shoulder and nodded. "Don't be late."

"I'll be back," I whispered.

Mr. Death must have heard me because he cackled in a way that said, *"No you won't. You'll never be back. Not to see her or your family or your friends ever again."* Then, without warning, he grabbed the collar of my shirt and started dragging me out the door, singing a familiar tune. "We're off to see the carnival! The wonderful Underworld carnival!"

When I glanced over my shoulder, Mrs. Stiltskin mouthed, *I'll find you.*

I'd heard those words once before. While her intentions were good, it was the same thing I'd been promised by Hunter. And my parents. And neither of them had found me yet. I was beginning to wonder if they ever would. I'd have to figure this out myself.

Mr. Death's grasp was strong, and I needed to break free. I wriggled, careful not to tear off any other body parts. "Not so fast. You've got work to do."

"I know." I needed to sound cooperative, so I changed the tone of my voice. "And I'll do it. But it'll be easier if you just let me walk by your side."

Mr. Death sized me up, probably wondering if I was trying to trick him.

"C'mon." I threw my hands into the air. "It's not like I can leave."

His shoulders relaxed. "Fine. But if you try anything—"

"I won't," I said resolutely. "Like I said, I can't leave. Where would I even go?"

"Smart girl."

Yup, I thought. He was about to find out just how smart.

Chapter 29

We arrived at the Underworld Carnival, mostly unscathed. Well, Mr. Death looked the same, but I had a few new missing pieces of flesh that had just decided to fall off. Plus, my stomach decidedly disagreed with life in the Underworld and those scrambled brains. I couldn't be sure if I was hungry or had a bug. The growls and gurgles sounded like a conversation between demons.

I still didn't have a plan as to how I would escape, but I knew it would come to me eventually. There had to be a way out. There had to be laws against child labor. No way would I serve Mr. Death for eternity! Perhaps he had a weakness. There might even be some built-in flaw to the Underworld. Maybe even Mrs. Stiltskin would pull through for me and assist in my escape. Or my family and friends would come to my rescue. Or maybe, just maybe, I could do this on my own.

"You want me to work the Ferris wheel?" I rubbed at my arm, which felt as though it might fall off at any moment.

"Yes, you'll be doing your fair share!" Mr. Death's eyes narrowed into thin slits.

BRAIN FREEZE

Stinky: *Hey! Pass the popped brain corn. *scratches belly**
Slimy: *One second. Just let me get the melted motor cortex.*
Crawly: *Anyone feel like this is a bit like watching a cliché horror movie?*
Creepy: *Yesssss. This happenssssss every tiiiiime.*
Yucky: *It certainly does!*
Icky: *Why do we keep watching? *sneezes**
Steve: *Maybe because our little worm lives are so interesting.*
Yucky: *You mean boring. *yawns**
Stinky: **grabs handful of popped brain corn* Speak for yourself. *stretches and farts**
Steve: *Maybe we should help her.*
Slimy: *Why isn't she moving?*
Yucky: *Because Steve's leaning on the motherboard again.*
Steve: *Oh. Oops. Sorry about that.*

"Sarah." Mr. Death waved a clownish hand in front of my face. "Sarah White."

The worms froze my whole body as they munched away upstairs, having their odd little conversation.

"Sarah!" Mr. Death said sharply while he clapped his hands.

I blinked, snapping out of it. "What?" It felt like I'd just come out of a fog.

"My dear girl." He chuckled. "I think you just had your very first brain freeze!" He slapped a glove-covered hand against his knee, as he bent at the waist with a guffaw.

"First?" Little did he know I'd been having loads of them. And for quite some time now.

"Yes-sir-ee bob! And you'll have plenty more where that came from!" He leaned close and took my head in his hands. His breath smelled of rotten eggs. It made me want to puke. He peered into my ear. "Looks like you've got about, oh, seven worms"

"Yes. I know."

"You do?" He folded his arms in disbelief.

"Yeah, they've been talking..."

Mr. Death's eyes widened and something about it warned me not to mention another thing. Had to play it cool. "Whatever will I do? I can't have seven worms in my head!" I placed my arm against my forehead melodramatically.

"Hmmm..." Mr. Death tapped his chin.

"This is gonna be a real joy." I swallowed a lump that had risen to my throat. It landed rock hard in my stomach.

"Worms are a special and necessary addition." Mr. Death smirked as he rocked on his heels.

"So that worm wasn't kidding when he said he was squished in there with six others of his kind?" I played dumb so Mr. Death wouldn't suspect anything. Because sometimes it seemed like my worms were trying to help me, or maybe I could convince them to.

"Nope!" Mr. Death took a step closer. "I'll let you in on a secret, too." I held my breath so the stench from his mouth wouldn't knock me over. "They're a real party!" Mr. Death laughed like it was the funniest thing in the Underworld. "Be careful though. They can get a little annoying. One time I had a zombie working a carnival ride, and he got one of those nice, long brain freezes. You know the ones." He pointed a finger at my forehead. "Well, by the time he unfroze, the ride had been going for a full twelve minutes. Everyone on board had gotten motion sick, turned a shade of green and everything was covered in—"

"Okay! Okay!" I put my hands up to my ears. "I get the picture! Thank you very much."

BRAIN FREEZE

Steve: That's a great idea! Tell him you're sick.
*Stinky: Yeah, you've got a stomach ache. *rubs hairy belly**
Slimy: Yeah, tell him you don't want to short circuit the equipment by getting sick—
*Icky: Spare the details. We get the idea. *blows nose**
Steve: Then, as soon as he agrees, you can make a run for it.
*Icky: Just don't go back to the cottage. *rubs watery eyes**
Creepy: He'sssss bound to follow you therrrrrrre.
Crawly: The elevator! Heh-heh.
Steve: But she doesn't have the key.
*Yucky: You said butt. *laughs**
Slimy: We'll figure something out.
Steve: Just remember. You're sick.

I rubbed my belly. "Maybe I should just take a sick day. I'm not feeling so well." Summoning a half smile, I hoped he'd read the pathetic expression on my face. Pity was a surefire way to get off the hook.

"Nonsense! No one gets sick in the Underworld." Mr. Death pulled a lever. "You're dead, remember?"

"You know as well as I do that I didn't die. I fell through a mirror." My voice was calm despite the fact that I had anger bubbling deep in my gut.

"Oh, I know all about that."

I gulped. Of course, he did. "You sent it to me, didn't you?"

Mr. Death guffawed. "You know me so well and we've only just been introduced."

From the date on the newspaper I knew I'd been here a while. But I played dumb. "Hasn't it been an entire day since we met?"

"Hahaha!" Mr. Death laughed, throwing his head back. "It's been a bit longer than that. Another hour and…"

"And what?"

"Well, what do you know? Here we are." He placed one hand on my back while the other swung open a rusty gate. "Here's the ride you'll be monitoring. Largest Ferris wheel from here to Hades."

"Whoa." My neck ached as I strained to take in the full spectrum of the monstrosity before me.

Mr. Death guided me into a small open booth. A wooden L-shaped wall behind me displayed various posters with rules and regulations.

1) Two per seat, exceptions for ghouls and screaming banshees only.

2) Nooses buckled tightly around the neck.

3) All limbs, attached or detached, must remain inside the ride at all times.

4) Decapitation is not our responsibility, if this should occur, please collect your head at the end of the ride.

To my side was an electronic panel covered in a multitude of buttons and levers. Underneath the panel was a shelf with a few random tools; a screwdriver, hammer, nails, and a roll of duct tape.

"I'll show you how to work it. But only once!" His goofy clown grin made my skin crawl. Something about this entire exchange made me remarkably nervous. "Now, Sarah," he said, his voice lowering an octave and becoming ominously quiet. "You press this button first, then pull the lever back. It's important you do it in order."

I nodded. "Button. Then lever. Got it."

"You must operate the ride continuously, only pausing to let old passengers off and new ones on. If you stop for too long, it'll be curtains for you," he said as he made a slicing motion with his finger across his throat. Then he leaned closer. "One last little reminder. The dead never leave the Underworld. EVER. And neither do the Living!" Dark shadows made his creepy clown face turn into a sinister portrait of evil. He grabbed the hammer from the shelf and raised it into the air, inches from my head.

FERRIS WHEEL

1. Two per seat, exceptions for ghouls and screaming banshees only.

2. Nooses buckled tightly around the neck.

3. All limbs, attached or detached, must remain inside the ride at all times.

4. Decapitation is not our responsibility. If this should occur, please collect your head at the end of the ride.

Chapter 30

Mr. Death swung the hammer. It narrowly missed my head and slammed against a nail in the wall behind me. He backed away and the shadows disappeared. "Have a good day on the job!" He meant this in the most sinister way. I was sure of it. The shadow's steps were just out of time with his own as he hobbled away.

BRAIN FREEZE

Slimy: She's lucky that wasn't her head.
Yucky: That would have been a sight.
Steve: What do you mean she's lucky? We're in here, too.
Creepy: Weeeee would have been mussssssh.
Crawly: Yup. Mush. Heh-heh.
*Stinky: Did someone say mush? Sounds delicious. *burps**
*Icky: What is she waiting for? *sneezes**
Steve: Sarah, time to get out of here. Go home!
Slimy: You're leaning on the motherboard again, Steve!
Steve: I'm going to need to fix that.

"Strange," I muttered, coming out of the trance-like state. I rapped my knuckles against my temple. "What are you weirdos doing in there? We need to find a way to get home, so stop making my brain mushy."

Icky: Yes! Home! *blows nose* Maybe I can finally get rid of this cold.
Slimy: We've only been waiting an eternity for you to say that.
Icky: You want me to get rid of my cold?
Creepy: Nooooo. We don't caaaaaare about your coooooold.
Crawly: We want Sarah to find her way home. Maybe. Heh-heh.
Steve: If you stop talking, maybe she can follow through with it.
Stinky: I need more popped brain corn if I'm going to sit through the rest of this. *slurps soda*
Slimy: I think you broke the control panel, Steve.
Steve: Not again.

"Whoa. That was strange." I scratched my head as my gaze fell to my feet. "What was I doing? Was I supposed to go somewhere?" Riders screamed on the giant Ferris wheel and I blinked. "Oh right. I have to operate this ride."

Raven flew down and landed on my shoulder. "KOW!" he crowed. "CAW, CAW!"

The noise of his crowing snapped inside my head and I suddenly remembered everything. It all came rushing back in an icy chill on my spine. Home. I needed to get home. I whirled around. Ready to leap off the platform, I noticed a small crowd had gathered at the ride entrance.

"Let us on!" one of the little ghouls screamed.

"Ssssh. Shhh!" I put a finger to my lips. I didn't need them drawing attention. If Mr. Death found out I was slacking already, I was done for. That's when an idea popped in my head. If the job did itself, then I could sneak out of here. All I'd have to do is figure out a way to get the ride to operate on its own. I'd outsmart Mr. Death and be reunited with my family in no time.

"Two per seat," I said as I swung the gate open and let them onto the ride. A banshee floated past. It screamed and then possessed one of the passengers. "Uh...excuse me. I said two per seat. Banshee makes three."

"Not according to the poster," the possessed passenger said.

"You're absolutely right. Banshees are the exception." I smiled nervously. This place gave me the creeps, but I had to do my job until I could figure out my escape. Remembering the directions, I pressed the button then pulled the lever, holding it in position. The Ferris wheel creaked gloomily as it circled the passengers up and over and back around. "Some afterlife this is."

A few rotations later, I released the lever and the ride screeched to a halt. Ghouls and boys of all shapes and sizes got off and began wandering around the carnival grounds. "Have a nice day," I called to them, realizing I sounded a bit too much like Bert. One child came up, snapping and snarling, showing abnormally large teeth, and I stumbled backward. "Whoa, whoa, back off, tiger."

Some of the children glowed faintly, like fairies, and

others seemed to lack light completely, like a forlorn emptiness. Most of the creatures looked human, but there were some that reminded me of apparitions from my childhood nightmares. They might try to suck your soul. The ones with extra limbs, or oddly colored blue skin and gills were more like curiosities than anything to be afraid of.

BRAIN FREEZE

Steve: Sarah, why are you still operating this?
Creepy: Yeaaaaah. You need to ssssssneak away.
Steve: Let everyone on the ride. Keep it running and then you can take off.

"That's exactly what I had planned." I turned around and called out, "Ride the Ferris wheel! One ticket each. Ride or die!" I laughed but no one paid attention to me. Everyone seemed pre-occupied with a popcorn stand promising freshly popped brain corn.

I suddenly had a very strange craving for another serving of Mrs. Stiltskin's cooked brains. Which made me realize that her brain food really did work! I hadn't fallen apart in hours!

Panic rose inside my chest as I also realized if the ride was stopped for too long Mr. Death would grow suspicious. Then I might never get out of here.

What if I was stuck in the Underworld forever? Surrounded by freaks and ghouls? I had to get the undead on my ride and fast!

"Ferris wheel! Get your slow, dizzying Ferris wheel!" I called. Where was a megaphone when you needed one?

A few of the children lifted their heads, easily distracted from the popcorn. They tugged at the adults until they gave in and gathered at the entrance, like minnows in a tide pool.

"Phew! That was a close one." I wiped a bead of sweat from my upper lip.

BRAIN FREEZE

Creepy: Let them riiiiiide.
Steve: Then you can sneak off.
Crawly: Hurry! Heh-heh.
Steve: It's your perfect opportunity to get away.

"I think you're right. Now's my chance," I whispered. After the ride filled, I pressed the button and pulled the lever. The Ferris wheel growled to a start, its gears shrieking with each rotation. I swiped the duct tape and strapped the lever in place. It would hold just long enough for me to get away. "I'm leaving right now."

"Oh, you are, are you?" a disembodied voice whispered.

Chapter 31

The hairs on the back of my neck stood on end and I froze, standing stiff as an ice pop. I had been caught. This was the worst possible scenario!

I'd never be able to leave the Underworld.

I'd be a prisoner forever, doing a meaningless job.

I'd never celebrate my thirteenth birthday.

I'd never see my friends or family again.

Nodding slowly, I stuttered. "Y…y…yes."

"Probably not without my help."

"Your help?" My throat was dry, but I squeaked out the words.

A wrought iron fence topped with black skulls acted as a barricade between the Ferris wheel and the edge of the carnival. Beyond the fence, was a hedge of bushes which rustled like they were being attacked. "It's me." Mrs. Stiltskin popped up, waving her arm.

I breathed a sigh of relief. Mrs. Stiltskin had returned to help me, just as she had promised she would. It really was my chance to escape. "Eeeee! I'm outta here!"

"Quietly," she whispered. "We don't want anyone to notice."

"Good point." I nodded and stretched, acting tired like

a good employee after a long, hard day of work. Letting the ride spin and spin, I stepped off the platform. Raven seemed to understand my plan and watched as I wandered casually alongside the Ferris wheel towards the fence line. Once at the bush, I pretended to observe the leaves of the plant.

Raven flew directly over my head and landed in a nearby tree. He groomed himself while staring down at the bushes. To anyone watching, they would have seen this as natural bird behavior. But I knew he was ready to help me escape any way he could. "You're quite the actor, aren't you?" I whispered to Raven.

The bird nodded.

As soon as I was sure no one was watching, I darted into the bush. "Mrs. Stiltskin!" I threw my arms around her. "You came! I knew you would!"

She hugged me back and smoothed my hair. "Listen. I have some bad news."

Nothing could be worse than what I'd already been through. Except maybe being stuck here forever. "It can't be that bad."

"I'm not so sure about that." She lowered her head. "I tried to make a potion to help you, but my magic doesn't work so well anymore. It's not potent enough but it's worth a try."

"Magic? What are you talking about?"

"Never mind that." She grabbed my hand and placed a small, oval shaped bottle in my palm. Green liquid sloshed around inside the container. Mrs. Stiltskin pulled the cork from the top, pushing the bottle to my lips. "Drink it quickly."

"It smells like rotten eggs." I snarled my lip in disgust but threw my head back anyway. The medicine went down in a single gulp. Which was a good thing since the taste was as awful as it smelled.

"I hope it works, because if it doesn't, then I'll have to figure something else out. There's no choice." Mrs. Stiltskin paused. "We need to get you out before sunset, or it'll be too late."

I ran my fingers through my hair, tucking a strand behind my ear. "No, it has to work. Maybe we could—"

"Is that…is that what I think it is?" Mrs. Stiltskin's eyes grew wide.

"What?"

She grabbed my wrist. "It's the—"

"Bracelet." A smile tugged at my face as I thought about it. "Cindy gave it to me for my birthday."

"No. Not that." Mrs. Stiltskin laced her fingers around the metal charms. "This." She held up the key.

"Oh right. That's from Cindy, too."

Mrs. Stiltskin laughed wildly. "Oh, that darling, darling girl!"

"I don't understand."

"Don't you see?" She unclasped the bracelet with the skeleton key from my wrist. "It's your way out."

Maybe being in the Underworld affected my ability to think clearly but this all felt a bit much to understand. "It is?"

"Don't you know what kind of key this is?"

I blinked. "It's a skeleton key!" I cried, suddenly realizing the significance. "It opens every lock."

Mrs. Stiltskin nodded.

But how could a skeleton key help me here? Was there a door that could lead back to the real world? Questions buzzed in my head. And so did something else.

BRAIN FREEZE

Steve: Thank heavens someone's got this figured out!
Slimy: Good thing because I was getting a little fried.
Icky: *achoo!* No one likes fried worms.
Crawly: Heh-heh. That's a good one!
Steve: Would you all knock it off? This girl has very little time to escape. We can't be responsible for her demise.
Slimy: Then you should probably stop leaning on the motherboard.

Steve: Dagnabbit!

"Are you all right?" Mrs. Stiltskin yanked on my sleeve.

I rubbed my forehead and nodded. "I think so."

"You seemed to drift away....oh no!" Mrs. Stiltskin peeked in my ear. "You're not having brain freezes, are you?"

Those darn worms. "That's what Mr. Death called them, too."

Mrs. Stiltskin gasped and stepped back. "He knows?"

I nodded, feeling suddenly very sick to my stomach.

"I thought we had till dusk, but it might be too late." Mrs. Stiltskin shook her head.

"No, it's not. Don't lose hope. I haven't." I grabbed the charm bracelet from her and held it into the air. "Cindy wouldn't give up either. She'd find the good in the situation somehow." My head ached but I shook the pain away.

Mrs. Stiltskin stared at me, her jaw slack as a tear rolled down her cheek. "You're right." She took me by the hand. "There's no time to waste. We need to go now."

Just as we were about to dart off, a twig snapped, and we froze. Mrs. Stiltskin's eyes went wide as my necklace suddenly began to glow. She steadied herself, breathed deeply and knelt on the ground. There was something lurking nearby. I knew it. My necklace knew it. And Mrs. Stiltskin did, too. She grabbed my shoulders and squeezed them. "Listen carefully," she whispered. "You run. You run as fast as you can." She swirled me around and pointed into the distance past the ticket booth into a space I'd never seen before. "There will be a pink elevator waiting for you—"

Another twig cracked, snapping us to attention. We both seemed to hold our breath. Mrs. Stiltskin put a finger to her lips, glancing once again into the distance. "Use the key. It'll open the door." Her low, whispered voice was barely audible. "The elevator will take you..."

My necklace pulsed.

"Now go!" She pushed me and I stumbled forward. Then I bolted like lightning, regretting my failure to get more information. What was the final destination of the elevator?

Mrs. Stiltskin's screams flooded my ears as a loud crash came booming down. My eyes welled with tears. But I didn't look back. I couldn't.

Chapter 32

L egs aching, I ran straight past the ticket booth. Bert's slow voice hollered a warning, but it didn't stop me either. I kept running, just like Mrs. Stiltskin had instructed.

Flashing lights bounced on the horizon. "That... must...be it," I panted. "Just a little further." As I rounded a turn, large bulb-like lights lit up a bright pink elevator. "There it is!" Excitement overcame me, but my head pounded harder than ever.

BRAIN FREEZE

Slimy: She's almost there.
Yucky: She's gonna make it!
*Icky: *blows nose* Well she would have.*
*Stinky: *burps* Why is she stopping now?*
Steve: If you would stop talking, she might be able to get there.
Creepy: You mean our talking stops her from doing stuff?
Slimy: Only when Steve is sitting at the controls.
*Steve: Not again. *face palm* Now be quiet.*

The pain stopped and I blinked. Where was I? What was I supposed to be doing? My hand ached and I opened my fist. I'd been squeezing a key and it left an indentation in my palm. I glanced ahead spying an elevator. None of this made sense. I peered back over my shoulder, only to see a shadow creeping closer. My necklace lit up in warning. *Shadow bad*, I thought. My heart gave a sudden, indignant thump sending my breath into uneven waves. I needed to get out of there. And I needed to do it fast.

"What are you waiting for?" a familiar cranky voice said.

"Cheddar!" I squealed. "I'm so happy to see you!"

"No time for that." The mouse harrumphed. "Would you get over here already?" He waved his little mouse hand, gesturing toward the elevator.

That's it! The elevator was my escape out of the Underworld. "I'm coming!" He didn't need to send me another invitation. Panting, I sprinted, leaving the shadow in the distance. When I reached the door, it was locked. Searching for a way in, I ran my hand over the surface. Nothing. Panicked, I looked at Cheddar. "Can't you open it?"

"Well, well. The Living. Always wanting assistance. You want me to do everything?"

"Yes. I mean no." I shook my head. "How do we open it?"

"I'm just a mouse, so what do I know? But I think that a key would be useful." Cheddar folded his little skeleton arms across his chest.

Too many brain freezes were getting to me. "The key!" My heart pounded.

"Do you have one?" Cheddar tapped his foot.

"Yes!" Excited, I jumped up, throwing my hands over my head. The key slipped out, hitting the side of the elevator before bouncing off into the grass.

Cheddar humpfed. "You *had* one."

"No, no, no, no!" Sinking to my knees, I felt around in the grass.

"I believe the correct answer is yes." Cheddar scurried up my arm. "You'll never make it out now."

"Thanks for the vote of confidence."

Cheddar sat on my shoulder. "Anytime."

"Well are you just going to sit there or are you going to help me?"

"The Living. Always needing help." He scurried back down and into the grass.

"Thank you." The shadow encroached and I swallowed hard. We needed to find that key and fast!

"Yeah, yeah." He shook his fist. "But this is the last time." His tail twitched as he grumbled under his breath. Something about always getting humans out of a fix and that he better not need to reassemble his bones this time.

"I promise. No one wants that more than me." I was certain, more than ever, that I never wanted to return to the Underworld if I ever made it out alive.

"Found it!" Cheddar's voice filled with glee. "Found it, found it, found it!"

"You got the key?"

"No." He poked his head up, holding something very small in his bony fingers.

"What is it?"

"One of my phalanges." He snapped his finger into place. "It's been missing ever since Cindy—"

"What do you mean?" Discreetly, I glanced at my own pinky still taped to my hand, wondering if I'd eventually become like Cheddar.

"Forget it. Just never you mind. The living…"

"Yeah, yeah, The Living, Schmiving. I get it. You're unhappy. Well, you're not the only one that's miserable. If I don't get out of here, something very bad will happen to me. I really don't want to find out what that is." I glanced over my shoulder at the shadow making steady gains. "So, if you would stop complaining about every little thing you don't like and help me out then maybe your life…er… undead life wouldn't be so miserable."

Whoa. That felt good.

Cheddar tipped his head in that inquisitive way animals do when they're trying to understand something. Then he scurried off without so much as a goodbye.

Oh no! What had I done? Serves me right. I shouldn't have said something so terribly mean, even if it felt gratifying. When would I ever learn to be nice?

There wasn't time to make amends. If I was going to save myself, then I'd have to find that key all on my own. Sensing the shadow, and hearing the footsteps, I continued to grope around in the grass. Sweat rolled off the tip of my nose and dripped onto the ground. I'd find that key and I'd get out of the Underworld if it was the last thing I did. Dirt caked my nails as I raked through the soil. It was here. I just knew it. It was only a matter of finding it before the shadow found me first.

Rocks and twigs rained behind me as I tossed them

over my shoulder in search of the key. My hand stumbled upon a cold piece of metal. Parting the grass, I saw the shiny shank. "They key!" I grabbed it and rushed to the elevator. "Now to just figure out how this works…"

"I can show you," a voice cackled.

The hairs on my arms stood on end. I turned around and there he was. Mr. Death.

"But first, I'll need your LIFE."

Chapter 33

My fingers fumbled with the key. I couldn't let him take me or steal my life. Or what was left of it, because I had a horrible feeling there wasn't much remaining, even if I did escape the Underworld.

Mr. Death cackled as his shadow crept closer. "You'll never figure it out."

I would. I had to.

"Time is running out for you, Sarah." His voice inched nearer, threatening me with each syllable.

I'd find a way out before he got to me. There had to be a way. I just needed to locate the keyhole, but it seemed invisible. As I brushed my hand across the surface of the elevator, I found it.

"There's no use in trying." Mr. Death's large cold shadow chilled me like a harsh winter day without a coat. "You'll never escape."

Throwing a glance over my shoulder, I shivered at his slow steady march, his confident, cunning words.

"You'll be trapped here forever."

My fingers fumbled as I wiggled the key into the lock. *It's in!* The elevator door opened. Mr. Death's hand swiped at me as I leapt inside the elevator. The door slammed hard, shutting him out. Mr. Death's angry face—lit with malice and hatred—appeared in the glass of the door, staring me down. "I'll get you next time!" he roared.

"Well, that was a close one."

I leapt back. "Cheddar?"

"You're welcome." He pressed a button that said L.L, which I hoped didn't mean Lower Level because I was as low as I wanted to go.

"I'm sorry for everything I said. It was rude and…"

Cheddar flicked his tail. "Forget about it."

I knelt down and scooped him into my hands. "How did you get inside?"

"That's one of my specialties. Sneaking around when no one expects it."

"I'd have to agree with that. I had no idea you were there."

The elevator ascended as slowly as a turtle in molasses. I glanced out of the window again, but Mr. Death had disappeared into the night of the Underworld. "He's gone," I said to Cheddar. "He sure left in a hurry, too." There was an audible sense of relief in my voice as the words came spilling out.

"That's not necessarily a good thing." Cheddar twitched his tail before scurrying over my shoulder to peer out the window.

"It's not?" My brow furrowed. His concern didn't make much sense. I thought I was safe once I got inside the elevator.

Cheddar pressed some buttons. "Can't this thing go any faster?"

"What's the hurry? We'll be there in a minute." Wherever 'there' was. In fact, if anything, I felt my stomach bubble at the uncertainty of where I was headed. Surely Mrs. Stiltskin wouldn't send me somewhere unsafe or unfamiliar. Would she?

The elevator creaked to a stop and the doors opened. The sky lit in a dim haze. Shades of orange and pink gave everything an eerie glow. If it was dusk or dawn, I couldn't tell, but one thing I did know; I was somewhere unfamiliar. And it most certainly felt unsafe. Because when I stepped out onto the earth surrounding the elevator, I was in a cold, grave-filled cemetery.

A shudder rolled across my arms. "Why would she send me to a cemetery?"

"The Living! Always so scared of the deceased."

"I'm not afraid of the diseased." Through my chattering teeth and the shiver suffocating my body, I gave Cheddar a stern look.

"Not diseased. Deceased. The Dead." He stood up on his hind legs, rubbing his front paws together. "You've already walked amongst the dead. Why would a cemetery scare you?"

For once, the little rodent was right. "How do I get home?"

"Don't you recognize this place?" Cheddar scurried toward a tree where he found an acorn.

A breeze swept my hair into my face and as I brushed it behind my ear, I noticed a white headstone directly to the side of the elevator. The fact that it was a cemetery was obvious but....which one? Shrugging I said, "Not really."

"Look close," Cheddar said, pointing to the headstone.

The writing was clear. "Mrs. Stiltskin!" It was Cindy's mother's grave.

"Parkview Cemetery." Cheddar popped the top off the acorn just like a squirrel would do.

"Parkview!" I blinked. "I'm almost home!"

Cheddar nibbled on the acorn as a little worm squiggled out. Clearly the treat was rancid. "What are you waiting for?"

Creepy: Hey look! It's cousin Limpy!

I tapped my head making my worm quiet down.

Cheddar twitched his tail in enjoyment anyway. "The Living. Always needing an invitation."

I scooped the mouse into my hands, lifted him to my lips, and kissed his skull. "Bye Cheddar." A strange feeling grew inside my chest and it burst out of my eyes.

"Now don't start leaking on me." He dropped the acorn and folded his little mouse arms against his little mouse chest. "I never did like baths."

I stroked the mouse's head, feeling grateful for all the sacrifices he made on my behalf. "Thank you for everything." My voice quivered with the sob I held back. The same sob threatening to turn me into a blubbering, emotional wreck.

"Humpf. You're welcome," he said gruffly. But was that a tremble in his voice?

I kissed his head again. "I'll never forget you." I sniffled.

"Now don't get sentimental on me." A tear formed near his eye socket and I wiped it away. "And don't you dare go telling anyone about that. I have a reputation to uphold."

"I won't." I made an 'X' across my heart then held up my fingers in an oath of promise.

"Good." He shook his body, from head to tail, as if he were a dog recovering from an unwanted bath. "Now get going!"

I placed him back on the ground near the elevator. "Travel safe."

Cheddar nodded and, in a flash, both he and the elevator were gone.

"Mom and Dad will be so happy to see me," I whispered between pants as I ran home. "I wonder if they've missed me as much as I missed them." I nearly stopped in my tracks as I thought about Rose. Did she miss me, too? Did she miss sharing a room with me? Or that we'd always fought because we were so different?

That wasn't important now. I had to get home. Sleep was needed in order for these strange headaches and brain freezes to go away. Even though Mr. Death was in the Underworld, I felt I should warn my family about him. They probably wouldn't believe my story, but I had to tell them. Because, for some reason, I couldn't help thinking that I hadn't seen the last of him. And that this wasn't over. Not by a long shot.

Birds chirped their melodious tunes welcoming the new day. It was a welcome sound. Things I'd taken for granted before were the things I'd missed most in the Underworld.

I burst through the front door just as the sun peeked over the horizon. "Ma-um! Da-ad! I'm home!" The door slammed shut behind me. As I stood in the middle of the living room, the house felt cold and eerily quiet. No sounds of Mom working in the kitchen. No rustle of Dad's newspaper. No cries from Tommy. Hands sweating, I ran into the kitchen. No evidence of last night's dinner. No cold breakfast on the counter.

Returning to the living room, I called upstairs. "Hello? Anybody home?" Maybe they were still sleeping. My feet carried me up the flight of stairs so quickly they almost didn't even touch the ground. When I reached the landing, I paused, realizing that I didn't want to wake them if they were still sleeping. Despite the anxious feeling pulsing through my veins, I tiptoed down the hall to my parent's room. I peered inside. "Mom? Dad?"

The bed was rumpled and lumpy. They were still sleeping! A sigh of relief burst through my lips. I tiptoed closer. They'd be okay if I woke them, wouldn't they? Wouldn't they want to know I had returned, safe and sound?

Of course, they would!

Slowly, I reached my hand out and placed it on the bedding. I squeezed. "Mom." But instead of a firm shoulder, I felt something soft. "Mom?" I tore the covers back and gasped.

My parents were missing!

Chapter 34

"Nooooo! No, no, no!" I fell to my knees and cried. Where were they? What happened to them? Didn't they miss me?

I ran down the hall to Tommy's room. "Tommy? Tommy, Tommy!" But he didn't respond. I slid into his room and saw an empty crib. My baby brother was gone, too.

Feeling the emotions knot my insides together into a lump of tangled knitting yarn, I tiptoed to my room. The closed door stared at me like a blank slate of possibilities. The possibility that my sister remained while everyone else had left.

"Rose?" I called, my voice barely above a whisper, the cotton ball in my throat choking off the sound. "Are you there?"

The door wailed as I pushed it open. The room looked as though it had been ransacked. Blankets torn off the beds. Clothes strewn everywhere. A broken vase leaked water onto the hardwood floor and the half-dead daises from Hunter were wilted and dry, their pathetic faces begging for nourishment. The ceiling had two arrows lodged in it, but her bow was missing.

My eyes were quickly drawn to the mirror in the

corner. I couldn't stand to look at it and quickly threw a sheet over it. That stupid mirror was the cause of all my problems. It had sent me to the Underworld and now my entire family was missing. I wasn't going to allow the mirror or Mr. Death to control my life or my future anymore.

I grabbed a jacket from the closet and prepared to head out in pursuit of my family.

Creepy: You'll neveerrrrr fiiiiiind theemmmm.
Crawly: Nope. Never. Heh-heh.

Steve: Would you two be quiet? You can do it, Sarah.

"Thank you, Steve," I whispered, trying not to let the negative worms affect me. Before I closed the door behind me, I heard a strange vibration. Peering over my shoulder, I saw Dad's cell phone on the table. Its screen lit up.

"Hello? Hello?" I shouted into the phone but there was no answer on the other end. Just a strange little cackle. My necklace glowed in the reflection of the window. "Mr. Death?" I gulped. How did he know my dad's cell phone number?

"Bwhahaha!" The laugh drilled into my eardrum and I quickly ended the call.

That's when I saw all the outgoing calls dad had made. Cindy's cell phone. Mort and Drac. Hunter. And the final call to 9-1-1.

I quickly dialed Cindy's number but there was no answer. Then Hunter. Again, no answer. Mort and Drac came up empty, too. Where was everyone? What had happened?

My pulse quickened and beads of sweat dripped from my brow. My stomach lurched. This was way too upsetting. My stomach lurched. Maybe I was getting sick. I pulled tissues from the box on the table and wiped my forehead as I collapsed on the couch. A fever made its way through my veins and I trembled violently. This was a weird flu of some sort. Maybe I'd caught it while I was in the Underworld.

BRAIN FREEZE

Steve: Get up. Get up and go!
Creepy: Yesssssss. You neeeeeeed to fiiiiiind themmmmm.
Icky: No. You need to stay home and rest your head. *blows nose* I hope I didn't contaminate you.
Yucky: I think you did.
Crawly: Well, she's a goner anyway. Heh-heh.
Stinky: Just like my last meal. *burps*
Steve: Sarah, you need to try. Get up!

At least one of my worms was right and I needed to listen to him. I needed to get up, just like Steve said. I had a feeling Creepy was just all talk. But I needed to try. I had to find my family no matter how sick I was. I'd find them or I'd die trying.

Squeezing Dad's phone in my palm, my eyes flooded with tears. "I'll find you. I promise I will." It was what they'd told me. Even though they hadn't followed through on their word, I forgave them. How could they have searched for me in the Underworld? Would they have even known to look for me there? "You can do it, Sarah. Just get up and move." Having no direction or plan, I rose to my feet and stumbled out the door. Thinking was over-rated, even if it would help me now. My family was missing, and I couldn't just sit here and do nothing.

Staggering down the porch steps out onto the lawn, Dad's phone rang again. The vibration sent shivers over my skin.

The display read, "Caller unknown."

I answered. "Hello?"

Another cackle. "Tee-hee, hahaha!" Mr. Death's shrill laugh made my ears burn.

He knew where I was.

"You don't scare me!" I shouted into the phone. "Stop calling this number!" I pressed the end button so hard my index finger ached. Thank heavens it didn't break off the way my pinky did in the Underworld. That would have been horrible!

Then it dawned on me. Maybe Mr. Death wasn't after me at all. Maybe he had been after my family the whole time!

Chapter 35

A cackle rang in the clouds. It rustled the branches of the trees. It boomed in everything around me.

Mr. Death was here.

He'd found a way out and if Mr. Death was as crazy as I thought, who knew what he'd do to my family if he found them first.

There needed to be a way to protect my family. The phone vibrated again, and I glanced down at the empty screen. Dad had made calls to Cindy, Hunter, and Mort and Drac. But he'd made another call. I scrolled through his call history. 9-1-1. That's it! I bet they were at the police station!

Even though my feverish body felt extraordinarily tired, I sprinted as fast as I could. Oh, how I wished I had some change for a taxi.

Steve: *Never mind that. You can do it.*
Creepy: *Nooooo she caaaaaan'tttttt.*

Steve: She can. And she will.

"C'mon Sarah." I put one foot in front of the other. "You've been through worse. You can handle a few blocks to the police station."

Stumbling all the way to the police barracks, my body threatened to give out at any moment. I never thought I'd be so happy to enter a law enforcement facility, but I finally felt safe. There wasn't time to waste, so when I didn't see my parents in the waiting room, I went to the reception area. A woman sat at a desk staring at a computer screen, ignoring the incoming calls.

"Can I help you?" she asked without looking up from her screen.

"I'm trying to find my parents," I said, my voice scratchy, breath like fire. I hoped I didn't have strep throat.

"You're lost?" The woman still refused to look up. She shoved a paper across the counter. "Just fill out this form."

"No. You don't understand," I said. "I'm not lost. My parents are."

"Well that's just ridiculous," she said finally breaking her gaze from her computer game long enough to shoot me a dirty look. "Fill out the form."

"Fine," I said. "But I'll need a pen."

The lady pointed to a paper-wrapped tin-can loaded with gaudy pens embellished with clown-like pompoms.

Quickly scribbling in the required information, I passed the paper back over the counter. "Now can you help me find my parents?"

"So, you really *are* lost!" The woman's face lit like a pumpkin on Halloween.

"Yes. That's it. I'm lost. Now can you help me?"

"Well, why didn't you just say so?" She took the form and read it. I watched her eyes scan the page. They stopped suddenly. She gasped. "Sarah? Sarah White?"

I nodded. "Yes, that's me."

She reached across the counter and grabbed my wrist. "You've had a lot of people worried, little girl."

"I'm sure." Probably not as worried as I was for myself. Or for my family if I didn't find them before Mr. Death did.

The woman led me down a poorly lit hall, the fluorescent light flickering overhead, to a small room. An officer sat at a desk, his head down as he scribbled notes on a yellow pad of paper. A couple sat in chairs facing him, their backs to me.

Her short, curly, dark bob was unmistakable. And the man's graying hair was none other than my dad's.

"MOM! DAD!" I shouted as I bolted into the room with my arms open.

They swiveled around in their chairs.

"Oh, my goodness! Sarah!" Mom leapt up. Her eyes were swollen and red with long-dried tears.

Dad opened his arms wide. "We're so glad you're home." I flew into his embrace, while Mom squeezed in, too.

"Where's Tommy?" I asked through tears. "And Rose?"

"The sheriff took them to the break room for a snack," the officer behind the desk informed.

"Thank you, Officer," my dad said.

"Yes. Thank you for bringing us our girl," Mom agreed.

But the officer hadn't done anything. I'd brought myself back. Found my family.

"Let's go home." Dad squeezed my hand.

"I'll get the other two," Mom said as she started out of the room.

"Wait!" I shouted after her. "I want to come, too."

Mom held out her hand. She led me to the break room where my siblings were enjoying a snack of chips and soda.

"Sarah?" Rose's eyes grew wide. She dropped her food and tackled me, snuggling her face into the crook of my neck.

She hugged me! Of all people, my sister hugged me.

"Are you okay?" Rose asked, her hot breath falling against my neck.

"I think so," I said. They didn't need to know I was coming down with something weird, like the flu or strep.

Tommy's arms wrapped around my legs. "Sarah dead!"

"No, Honey." Mom picked up Tommy. "Sarah was missing. But she's back now."

"Mirror make Sarah dead!" Tommy squealed.

Chapter 36

"Settle down, Tommy. The mirror didn't do anything to Sarah," Dad said, but it sounded like he was trying to convince himself as much as the rest of us. "Sarah was just missing for a while. But she's back now."

A shiver rolled down my spine. What if Tommy was right? What if the mirror had killed me and this illness was the first symptom? Maybe my parents should take me to the hospital just to make sure I was okay. No. No, that was ridiculous. The fever was playing tricks on me.

"Let's take her home," Dad said to Mom. "She looks exhausted."

Mom pressed her lips to my forehead. "And feverish. Vegetable broth and a nice long rest are in order."

When we arrived home, I was too tired for the broth. Instead I removed all the reminders of the Underworld, including Cindy's borrowed clothes, the bracelet, and Grandma Millie's necklace. Once in clean pajamas, Mom tucked me in bed. Her soft lips kissed my cheek. "Try to get some rest."

"You can tell us everything when you wake," Dad said while stroking my hair.

"I'm sure after a good sleep you'll feel much better. I'll

be up to check on you in a bit." Mom patted my feet before adding, "I'll have Rose sleep on the couch tonight."

"No." I shook my head, feeling a bit afraid to be alone and wanting my sister by my side. "I'd rather she sleep right there in her bed."

Rose smiled. "Are you sure? You know I snore loud. I don't want to keep you up."

"I'd probably sleep through it," I mumbled, my eyes growing heavy with sleep.

Dad closed the blinds. Then he and Mom turned out the light before they slipped through the door, closing it behind them.

An entire day later, bright afternoon sun blazed in my window and I sat up, rubbing my eyes.

*Steve: *yawns* Good morning sleepy head.*
*Icky: *grabs tissue* Wait a minute. *rubs nose* My cold is gone.*
Creepy: Maybe that'sssss because we're not in Kaaaaansassssss anymore.
Crawly: Heh-heh. We're in the White house.
*Stinky: You mean where the president lives? *stretches and farts* That's cool, I guess.*
Steve: No. Not that white house. Sarah White's house. She's home!

"Are you still talking in there?" I couldn't believe I was still experiencing those stupid brain freezes from those nasty (but sometimes helpful) little worms. I thought they would have disappeared once I returned home.

Stumbling out of bed I went into the bathroom, splashed some water on my face, and noticed something very strange. The skin on my hands changed from a beautiful sun-kissed olive to a sallow-looking algae. Even my pretty pink painted-fingernails turned a shade of army green.

"They're green!" It was one of those terrified realizations where your throat chokes up and you want to scream but it comes out in a whispered squeak. That's when you know things have gone from bad to holy-cow-what-the-heck-is-happening worse.

"AhhandwahahahHaaaaanddddsg-g-g-gggggr-reeeeen!!!!" My brain and tongue refused to cooperate, and I stuttered nothing but nonsense. "The hands!" I gasped.

"The green…the…hands! Forest! Under. World." I breathed wildly trying to make sense of it. I slapped my cheeks and my breath slowed as I collected myself.

"Why. Are. My. Hands. Green?" I panted. "Why are you green?" I shook them in the air until they felt weightless. Holding them in front of my face, I stared at my sickly skin color. This was too overwhelming.

Maybe I had learned to deal with worms in my head, but green skin? No way! Everyone could see this. At least I could keep the voices to myself.

Suddenly, the color began to creep up my arms in a slow and steady march. When it reached my neck, it choked my throat, then it slid down my chest like an Olympic diver and squeezed my heart. I gasped but it was cut short, coughing and sputtering like the Small's antique car.

My face flushed an unhealthy shade of apple green.

Oh no! I was turning into the Wicked Witch of the West. Wait. I couldn't be a wicked witch like her. Besides, all the witches on the weather vane were already accounted for. What would I be? The Wicked Witch of the Northern Hemisphere? The Equator? Or…the North Pole? Then I'd be stuck with elves as my henchmen. And everyone knows that elves make terrible henchmen. Flying monkeys are great, of course. But elves? It would be impossible to deal with all of their holly, jolly tunes and incessant sing-song caroling. Maybe that's what I was. The Grinch!

I had to stop this before it got worse. The green hadn't

reached my thighs yet, so there was still time. But what would stop a strange—what was this anyway, a virus?—from spreading? Oh no! Was this because I told Cheddar I wasn't afraid of disease? How could I have gotten that so confused?

There were lotions and acne cream in the medicine cabinet. They didn't sound like it would help so I tossed them aside, letting them fall to the floor. Wait! Acne cream stopped zits in their tracks. What if this green skin disease was nothing more than acne gone horribly wrong? It was worth a shot.

I grabbed the tube from the floor and squeezed a generous amount onto my palm. Rubbing my hands together, I smeared the cream on my arms and torso. My reflection revealed a sickly, pasty-green monster.

As if on cue, from the other room, my iPod blasted the song, "What makes you beautiful." Despite the horror staring back at me, I couldn't help but laugh. I definitely wasn't beautiful. No one on the planet would ever believe it.

Including Hunter.

Oh no! What would he think?

And what about Cindy and Scarlet? Would they still be my friends?

My heart began to burn with an achy sadness. And then my chest and arms burned, too. The acne cream had set my skin on fire!

Chapter 37

"Yowzers!" I screamed. There should have been some sort of warning label. I picked up the tube. "Triple the strength of regular acne creams. They weren't kidding." I turned the tube over in my hands. "Warning! Discontinue use if burning should occur." Now they tell me. That would have helped five minutes ago.

Must. Stop. The. Burning! I turned the faucet on and immediately started splashing water on my chest and arms, but it made a smeary mess. The only option was to jump in the shower. As soon as I hopped in, I saw the clarifying shampoo my sister had bought when a recent dye job went awry. "I'll just rub the shampoo on my skin!"

The directions said to use a dime-sized amount, but I figured if a little should do a little bit of good, a whole lot would do me a whole lot of good. Dumping half the bottle onto a loofah, I scrubbed as hard as I could tolerate it. My skin burned, but not from the shampoo or acne treatment. It was raw from all the scrubbing!

Worse, I was still green!

And what was this?

It was spreading!

The awful color had passed my thighs and was closing in on my knees.

I had to do something fast.

"Let me in," Rose called from the other side of the bathroom door.

Startled, I slipped in the tub. "I...ummm...I'm in the shower!" Not only could I *not* let my sister see me like this, but I still had to figure out how to make the green go away. My hands fumbled with the shampoo bottle as I read the instructions aloud. "For best results, repeat. Follow with Clarifying Conditioner."

"What did you say?" Rose pounded on the door.

"Uh...I said, I'm in the shower. Be there in a minute!"

"Well hurry up," Rose said. She paused then added, "I mean, hurry up. *Please.*"

"I'm hurrying." If only she knew. Following the directions on the bottle, I lathered up again. But this time I let it stew. Mom says things always come out better when they have a chance to marinate. Well, technically she's talking about my favorite casserole, but I didn't see why it wouldn't apply to this, too.

After five minutes (and Rose banging on the door at least two more times) I rinsed off, letting the soapy bubbles swirl down the drain. But nothing changed. I was still green!

Steve: I knew she didn't make it out of the Underworld in time. It's all your fault!

Creepy: It'sssss not myyyyy fault. Blame hiiiimmmmm.

Crawly: Heh-heh.

Icky: Can't blame me. *coughs* I'm too busy with this cold. *blows nose*

Steve: I thought that went away.

Icky: So did I. *sneezes*

Stinky: *scratches belly* And all I was doing was eating. *burps*

Slimy: Looks like it's your fault, Steve. You're leaning on the control panel again.

I paused, forgetting what I was doing. My hands trembled. Green! Ahhhh! My hands were green! Whoa. Déjà vu! Why did I feel like I'd just gone through this? Oh wait. Because I had.

"Would you knock it off in there?" I tapped the side of my head. "You made me lose my train of thought."

BRAIN FREEZE

Steve: You were going to use the conditioner next.

"Oh right! The conditioner!" I rubbed my skull. "Thanks, Steve."

Pouring some into my palm, I took a deep breath and smeared it on my skin. "That ought to do the trick." I closed my eyes and waited. "This is it." After I rinsed, I opened my eyes. I couldn't believe what I saw!

The green had spread all the way to my toes! I leapt out of the shower, toweled off and stood in front of the mirror. That's when I saw the horror of horrors.

My face was green—and so was my hair!

In fact, my hair looked like stalks of asparagus, laying in stiff green clumps next to my face. What happened to me? My beautiful complexion and hair were nothing more than a moldy pile of mixed greens. No one would ever be my friend if they saw me like this. I was a total freak! My mom was the only one who could help me but decided against asking for her help. What would she think? She'd probably faint and then I'd have to take care of her. How could I possibly care for someone else when I was in such a predicament myself?

What could I do now? I needed help and pronto! There was only one thing left for me to do; get dressed, find my dad and have him fix it all. He would know exactly what to do. And he wouldn't pass out like my mom.

Before I lumbered out of the bathroom, I peeked out of the door making sure Rose wasn't there. Thankfully she must have given up because she was nowhere in sight. My towel dragged behind me as I walked, but my foot caught on it and I tripped, stubbing my toe in the process. A wail burst from my mouth. But instead of my normal high-pitched scream it was deep and growly sounding. Was my voice changing, too?

I fell to the ground clutching the sore toe, shivering and rocking in place. "Daaa…." I started to call out, but I realized that it sounded like a moan and I was beginning to think it was the only sound I could make. I stood up, determined to get to my room and finally ask my dad for help. But my toe was too sore, and I had to drag my foot behind me with each step.

Moan. Thud. Draaaag.

Moan. Thud. Draaaag.

Moan. Thud. Draaaag.

My heart stopped as I realized exactly what had happened.

I had become a zombie!

A limping, green, matted-haired zombie!

Chapter 38

I fumbled the rest of the way to my room, dressed quickly, and tumbled down the stairs. I seemed to be getting well acquainted with the flooring in our house, including the slate tiles at the bottom of the stairs. Slate is a type of stone, in case you didn't know. Stones are hard, particularly when you face plant directly on them. At least my skull cushioned the blow to the rest of my body.

BRAIN FREEZE

Yucky: Take it easy out there.
Crawly: Yeah. You trying to give us a concussion or something? Heh-heh.

I rubbed my face and caught a glimpse of myself in the reflection of the window. My face sure had taken a beating. A giant goose egg rose up on my cheek. In fact, was that blood I tasted? I stuck out my tongue. It was covered in red ooze and teeth marks. And it was swelling rapidly, too.

"What's all that commotion?" Mom called from the kitchen.

"Meee-uuuuh," I called nervously. But it came out more like an unenthusiastic moan, my swollen tongue slurring the sounds together.

"Try to keep it down. I've got a soufflé in the oven."

Sure thing, Mom. Don't mind me. I've just turned green, bruised my face and nearly impaled my tongue with my own teeth, but your soufflé is definitely at the top of my list of things to worry about.

I opened the front door, hoping to find my dad in the yard. He was the only hope I had left.

"Dinner's at six," Mom hollered as if I'd already left. "Don't be late."

My knuckles blanched white as they curled around the doorknob. As soon as I loosened my grip, the unnatural shade of green returned. Good thing, I suppose. I didn't need another finger falling off the way it did in the Underworld.

A bunch of kids from school were standing on the sidewalk. They looked at me with their jaws slack. Gasping, I slammed the door. Then I bolted the lock and tried to sprint up the stairs, but it was more like heavy-footed lumbering. My toe still ached. Each step was as if a mousetrap was snapping on it over and over again.

"Sarah!" Mom's voice had an edge to it as she screamed my name from the kitchen. The same edge she gets when she hasn't had enough sleep. Or when she gets a migraine. Or worse, when Dad finds her stash of chocolate and eats every last piece. "What did I tell you about being quiet?" As if reminding me was going to change the fact that I was green. Or that her soufflé had probably already fallen. No one likes it anyway. I don't know why she insists on making it, then complaining that it never comes out right when everyone turns their nose up at it. Can you blame us though? A soufflé tastes like rubbery cheese that's been in the microwave. Why can't she make hot dogs and mac and cheese like normal moms do?

When I reached the top of the stairs, I shuffled to my room and let the door slam behind me. Actually, my door wasn't really capable of closing on its own. So yeah, I slammed it. Do the details really matter that much?

A second later the door flung open and Rose barged in. Couldn't I have two seconds to myself? TWO SECONDS! She flopped on her bed without saying a word and I kept my back turned to her.

"I need a few minutes alone," I said, my tongue cooperating despite the recent impalement.

"Ermagerd." Rose's mouth dropped. "What happened to you?"

"I uh…" I couldn't explain it. What *did* happen to me? Obviously, I was a zombie, and something changed when I went to the Underworld. Still, I couldn't put my finger on exactly what it was, other than the obvious fact that my skin had turned green. But *what* caused it? I probably would never know. Maybe it was those brains Mrs. Stiltskin had me eat. Or the potion! Oh no. Why would Mrs. Stiltskin poison me? Or maybe she didn't intend to. She did say her magic wasn't as strong as it once was.

"You're green," Rose said, her jaw still unhinged as she sat on her bed.

"That's stating the obvious."

"Can I touch it?" Rose reached her hand out, but she furrowed her brow before quickly pulling away. "Oh. Maybe that's a bad idea. It could be...contagious."

"Like a virus?" Oh no! What if it was? Would I contaminate everything I touched? Would I infect my family? "No, no, no." I limped around the room in circles.

"Looks like you're the freak," Rose said with a laugh.

I stopped in my tracks. She was right. I was the freak. And for once in our entire sisterhood lives, she wasn't. I couldn't handle being a freak. Being different. I wanted my beautiful hair and my pretty face again. Not green skin, a gimpy gait, and asparagus stalk hair. I would never fit in like this. I needed to be my normal self! What would I do if Rose was the normal one at school and I wasn't? This was a complete role reversal and I would never be the same. Ever again.

Chapter 39

"**I** *am* a freak." I started to sit next to her but then remembered I might be contagious. Instead, I flopped on my own bed. "I'll never be normal again. Will I?" My voice trembled and my throat burned but I refused to cry.

"I don't know." Rose shook her head and shrugged. Her expression was soft. If I didn't know better, I'd almost say sympathetic. She lowered her eyes and kicked at a sock on the floor. "It's not so bad."

"You think it could be worse?"

"Sure. Just imagine, you could be..." She tapped her forehead like she was thinking then stumbled on various words. "Purple, bearded, freakishly tall, three-legged, part dog...." But her voice drifted off because none of those things sounded all that bad in comparison. She must have felt the same way.

"I guess," I said, trying to make her feel better for helping me out. She meant well and that's what mattered.

"Green is the new pink, you know," she said, her eyes brightening and a forced smile emerging on her face. She sat on my bed, her hands on her knees. "You could set a new trend."

"I suppose I could," I said with a frown, not wanting to

be the poster child for trend-alert green skin. "If witches were in, then I'd be all the rage."

"Well, I've behaved like one for thirteen years. I could teach you the matching attitude." Rose smirked. "You just have to be a jerk. Simple as that."

I lifted my gaze at Rose who seemed to be apologizing in a round-about way. "Yeah, well I suppose I deserved it."

"Nah, I kinda liked it when you told me I was a loser." She rolled her eyes.

"For the record, I was actually jealous of your confidence. It never bothered you what others thought. You just kept doing your thing. I wish I could be like that."

"You thought I was confident?" Rose laughed.

For some reason this seemed funny and I started giggling, too.

We glanced at each other and simultaneously fell back on the bed, laughing. After a long bout of giggles, my face aching and stomach hurting, I turned to Rose. "Thanks."

Rose smiled.

"For helping, I mean."

"I know." She squeezed my hand. "You're welcome."

"Being a teenage zombie has its perks." I stared up at the ceiling. It wasn't the green skin I was referring to. My sister didn't hate me anymore and that was the best thing that could have come from this. And maybe, quite possibly, she understood me. Or maybe it was me who finally understood her.

"Yes, it does." She rolled off the bed. "Now get some rest, ya freak!"

"Yeah, yeah." I curled up under the covers. Then teasing, I said, "Bet you still can't even get me, Kat-*miss*."

Rose's eyes widened. As she left the room, she snapped her archery tubing. "We'll see about that."

The band flew straight at me and I pulled the covers over my head just in time to hear it hit the blanket with a soft wallop. "Nice aim! You've been practicing!"

"Everyday!" Rose said with a laugh.

She'd improved, and I felt proud of her for it. Our attitudes did, too. Was it possible for my sister to be my friend? I believed so.

Things had changed with her, for the better. If it was a result of my green skin, I'd almost be willing to stay like this forever. Almost. Still, I couldn't tolerate this new look. There had to be a way to fix it, make it better.

Besides, my relationship with Rose wasn't dependent on the way I looked.

I texted Cindy.

Hey Chickeroo.

Hey Chickadee. She texted back immediately. Wanna go eat some greens?

What an odd thing for her to say. What did she even mean by that? There was no way she was inviting me to grab a salad. Cindy was all about the burgers. Did that mean she knew about my condition? If so, how did she find out so quickly?

BRAIN FREEZE

Stinky: Greens? *burps* Nah. Protein. That's what we want.
Yucky: And sweets.
Icky: I'd prefer some cold medicine. *achoo* It seems my relief was only temporary.
Steve: It's a psychosomatic illness.

My hands sweated as I debated texting her back. But I slipped the phone onto my nightstand, refusing to respond until I could figure this out. After my experience in the Underworld and with Mr. Death, I knew I needed to be careful. This could have been him trying to trick me.

One thing I knew for sure, I needed to return to normal, even if it meant going back to the Underworld.

Chapter 40

I must have fallen asleep again because I didn't remember much after that.

Sunlight poured in through my window alerting me of a new day. I couldn't believe I'd missed dinner. I was starving! When I stretched, I saw my green hands and remembered everything. I had to get rid of this awful curse! But I wasn't sure how I was going to do it other than getting back to the Underworld. And really, I wasn't sure how I'd transport myself there. There was the mirror, of course, but I wasn't willing to crawl through that strange cave again. Not when something in it wanted to eat me alive. Or dead.

Moaning, I slipped out of bed and into my rotting slippers. They were old and smelled like dirt, but I didn't mind.

Crawly: It's not like she has one anyway. Heh-heh.
Yucky: Zombie humor!

Downstairs, it was quiet. Mom and Dad weren't nearby, so they didn't see my new zombie look. Even though Dad would have been helpful, Mom would have freaked out. Once in the kitchen, I pulled my favorite box of cereal from the cupboard.

*Stinky: Brain o's Breakfast Bites! *BEEEELLCCHH* My favorite.*
Crawly: Guaranteed to satisfy your mortal cravings!
Creepy: Or immortaaaaaal.

After consuming what could only be considered enough cereal to feed a small nation, I climbed the stairs and returned to my room. Rose walked in a moment later. "You can't go to school like that."

I glanced at my clothes. There was nothing wrong with my outfit, other than the fact that I'd slept in it. I just needed to change out of my slippers and into a pair of shoes. "What's wrong with a floral shirt? It matches my green skin perfectly." I blinked, realizing what I'd said. "Ohhhh…"

"Let's put some makeup on you." Rose grabbed a cosmetic bag from her dresser.

"Good idea," I moaned. The moaning thing seemed to get worse from time to time. I figured it was a zombie thing but I'm guessing Mom would say it was a teenage thing.

"There," she said, standing back and admiring her work. "No one would ever know that you're a…"

"A zombie," I said finishing the thought for her.

She held up a small mirror. "You look like yourself again."

It was true. I did look like me again, but I didn't *feel* like me. At least not like the old me. The judgmental, dying-to-fit-in Sarah. But I also didn't feel like the zombie Sarah either. I felt like someone new entirely. Beneath the layers of makeup that made me look human, another piece of me wasn't quite so normal. I pulled at a stalk of matted hair. "What do we do about this?"

Rose pursed her lips. "Hmmm…." She glanced around the room. She swiped a knit beanie from her closet and carried it over like she'd won the lottery. She pushed a clump of my hair out of the way and tucked it under the hat. My ear began to tickle. "Holy moly!" Rose squealed.

"What's the matter?"

"You have something in your ear!" Rose looked as though she would faint.

"Oh…that?" I laughed nervously. "That's just my worms." I wiggled a finger into my ear. "Get back in there."

"Worms?" Rose's face turned the color of my skin. "And you talk to them, too?"

"It's okay. I've gotten used to them."

Rose grabbed my shoulders. "We need to tell Mom and Dad."

"No way." I shook my head. "I don't want to worry them. Besides, they're not a bother." Actually, they kind of were but it's not like I could do anything about it.

"As long as you're sure." Rose looked concerned but she quickly resumed dressing me up. "I know! A scarf. That's what you need. It'll tie the whole look together." She rifled through her drawer and pulled out a white infinity scarf with ball fringe. Rose placed it over my head until it fell in place around my neck. She turned me around to face the mirror and peeked over my shoulder. "Perfect."

"You're the best." I smiled at my sister's reflection. "Now let's go," I said as I walked out of the bedroom, down the stairs and through the front door. Out into the pouring rain.

"Be careful!" Rose said. "You don't want the rain to wash your make-up off."

"Good point!" I pulled my coat tighter around my neck, preventing the rain from soaking my clothes. The coat didn't help shield my face much, so I kept my head down.

Creepy: What aaaaare youuuuu up to, Sssssarah?

"Leave me alone, Creepy," I said to one of my worms.

"Are you talking to your worms again?" Rose asked.

"Yeah. But I've really gotta figure out..." My words drifted off, thinking about how I could get rid of this zombie-illness. When I looked up Rose was already at the end of the block.

"Hurry! You're going to miss the bus." Rose waved at me as she climbed the steps.

Limping faster, I hurried to the bus stop. I reached the stairs and looked at the driver.

"Hurry up! It's raining out!" the driver said crankily, also pointing out the obvious. "Haven't got all day."

"Thanks for waiting," I said, gimping my way to the back of the bus. When I reached my usual seat, someone was missing. Cindy. Maybe she was running late, and her dad was driving her to school. It wasn't the first time she'd missed the bus and it probably wouldn't be the last. Still, it sure felt lonely without her.

When we arrived at school, I shuffled along with the other students who were still half asleep. Thankfully that helped me look like I fit in. No one would be able to tell the difference between a zombie and a middle-schooler.

In math, a few of the kids fell asleep. The drool from their mouths left marks on their tests.

The worms wiggled in my head. "Ha ha! That tickles. Stop it!" I scratched my ear and the worms settled in. "Good worms." I patted the side of my head as if they were a dog.

The teacher glared from the front of the room. "I'm watching you." She pointed two fingers at her eyes and then at mine.

I put my head down, keeping my eyes on my paper. Literally. My eyeball popped out! A second later a worm squiggled free. "What the heck? Get back in there!" Looking around, I hoped no one would notice as I shoved both the worm and my eye back in place.

It was probably a good thing half the class was asleep on their tests. When I glanced at the exam and saw all the difficult equations, I understood why they were asleep. Obviously, I'd missed a lot when I was in the Underworld.

BRAIN FREEZE

Creepy: Weeeee can help youuuuuu with that tesssssst.
Crawly: Yes. We can see it. Heh-heh.
Stinky: Yup. *lifts leg to fart* Could give you the answers.
Steve: Sarah's better than that. She'd never cheat.

"Time's up!" the teacher shouted to wake up the sleeping students. One kid startled and knocked over his chair causing a loud clatter.

"Sorry," the boy mumbled. Looking at his blank paper, his eyes grew wide. He was probably sorrier that he was going to fail his test.

The teacher sighed dramatically.

When the bell rang, I trudged into the girls' room. I needed to make sure my makeup was intact. Couldn't have anyone notice that I was different. A freak.

But when I looked in the mirror, my eyes were crazed with hunger. Braaaiiiins. That's what I needed. In more ways than one. That Algebra test was HARD. My stomach growled as a girl ducked into a stall. Exiting quickly, I returned to the hallway. Unfortunately, I was surrounded by temptation. More brains.

No. No, no, no. I refused to crave brains. But I couldn't help it. I lifted my arms and followed a boy down the hall. My leg dragged as I limped after him, my mouth dripping with wads of drool.

Chapter 41

When I caught up to him, he turned and stared. "What's the matter with you?" He flung his backpack over his shoulder.

"B...b...brrrr," I stuttered.

BRAIN FREEZE

Creepy: Braiiinsssssss
Steve: Were you leaning on the control panel?
Crawly: Heh-heh.
Steve: Well at least it wasn't me this time.
Creepy: Let me repeat. Braiiinssssssss.

I shook my head, snapping out of the trance-like zombie state. "Brian?"

"That's my name." He rolled his eyes. "Don't wear it out."

"Haha. Ha. Hahaha." I scratched the side of my nose nervously. "Haha."

"What's that?" Brian's eyes narrowed as he leaned in

close, examining my face. "Is that a booger? Holy heck! That's a giant booger!"

Mortified, I grabbed a compact from my bag and looked at my reflection. Cheese and rice! It was one of my worms! It had wiggled out of my brain and down my nostril. "Get back in there," I said.

"Who are you talking to?" Brian asked.

"Oh. Ha ha. Hahaha. Just, you know, my hair. I have all these fly-aways." I patted my hat, like somehow that would fix the stray strands. I was really talking about my worms but maybe he'd fall for my lame excuse. I lifted the compact again making sure the worm had obeyed. He had. But during my nervous moment, I'd scratched off some of the makeup. My green skin was exposed! I froze, devastated.

Stinky: Hey, I'll eat that if you're not going to.
Yucky: It's her skin. Not a booger.
Stinky: Well, I'll eat that, too. *belches* I'm all out of freshly popped brain corn. A worm's gotta eat.
Steve: No one is eating anything. No boogers. No skin. No nothing. Got it?

When I unfroze, I noticed the gathering crowd. Kids stopped in their tracks and stared at me. Some of them pointed. Others laughed. Where were Cindy and Scarlet when I needed them? And where was Hunter? Why hadn't

I seen them at school? In fact, I hadn't seen them since my return from the Underworld.

"Booger girl!" someone shouted, breaking me from my thoughts.

I quickly threw a hand over my nose, covering my green skin.

"Get out of here!" A voice yelled. "Go on! Don't you have something better to do?"

"Rose?" I slung my bag over my shoulder with one hand, still shielding my face with the other as Rose wrapped her arm around me.

"You're going to take care of the booger face?" Brian taunted.

"You know what, loser?" Rose stepped into Brian's personal bubble.

Brian smoothed a hand through his slicked back hair as his cheeks flushed bright red. "Wh...wh...what?"

"There's only one booger face around here and that's you." Rose stood taller and pointed at Brian's nose.

Brian laughed. "Yeah. Well at least I'm not an archery wannabe."

Rose clenched a fist. "Well coach said you couldn't hit a stationary target if it were the size of the moon."

Brian clenched his jaw. "Yeah, well you suck."

"And you suck so bad you make lollipops jealous," Rose quipped back.

The crowd burst into an explosion of laughter. Brian limped away his ego deflated.

"C'mon." Rose squeezed her arm tighter around my shoulder. "Let's get you out of here."

My sister saved my life. My reputation. "Thanks," I said.

"Don't mention it." Rose heaved her bag onto her back. "Let's get you home. We can tell Mom you're still sick."

I nodded. "That's probably a good idea." Now I needed to figure out a way to change my fate. There was no way I would go back to school as some sort of brain-craving zombie freak.

"Are you all right?" Mom's voice was super high when we entered the house. "Sarah? Rose? Do you want to tell me what's going on? Did something happen at school? What's wrong?"

I grabbed a couple of tissues from the bathroom. While I had my mom's attention, I wiped away the rest of the makeup. "What do you think is wrong with me, Mom? Take a good, long look. I'm a zombie!"

"Oh my heck," Mom gasped as she saw my green skin for the very first time. She swallowed hard, searching for something to say.

Tommy pointed at my face. "Sarah dead!"

"Oh, Honey," Mom corrected Tommy. "Sarah's not dead. She's just got some sort of virus."

"Mirror make Sarah dead!" Tommy wailed.

"That's enough, Tommy. You'll make your sister feel bad." Mom hugged me. "You'll be all better in no time." She may have been trying to assure me, but I think it really was for herself.

"It might be best if she doesn't go to school until she's better," Rose chimed in. Mom gave her a look. "Just so she doesn't expose the other kids."

"Hmmm...That's a good idea," Mom agreed. "Why don't you go to your room and get some rest." Mom turned to go to the kitchen. "And Rose."

"Yeah?" Rose paused as she hung up her bag.

"Thanks for taking care of your sister."

"It's no big deal," Rose said. "C'mon, I'll help you to your room." Rose squeezed my hand. She really was my friend. She'd stood up to bullies for me.

Once in my room, I kicked off my shoes and slid my feet into my old, moldy slippers. "Do you wanna watch a movie?" When she didn't answer, I turned around. Rose had pulled the sheet off my mirror and stood there staring into it. "Hey! What do you think you're doing? Don't you know how dangerous that is?"

"Shhh!" Rose put a finger to her lips and cupped a hand around her ear. "Don't you hear that?"

Creepy: *Now she'sssss heaaaaaring thingsssss.*
Crawly: *Maybe she's turning, too. Heh-heh.*
Stinky: *I'm hearing something. *belly gurgles* It's called an empty stomach.*
Yucky: *Oh please. You're not starving.*
Icky: **hands over a snotty tissue* It contains protein. Fills you right up. *blows nose into a clean tissue**
Steve: *Knock it off. All of you. Something's going on and we better pay attention.*

"Hear what?" I stood super still but all I could hear were my worms squiggling around.

"That!" She pointed. "That right there."

"I think it's your imagination." Whoa. This was a familiar situation. Except a total role reversal.

"It's stopped." Rose dropped her hands.

I slipped on my favorite white robe, getting ready to curl up in bed. "I told you it was nothing."

"Well, I'm so sorry!" she said sarcastically. But she still stared at the mirror, not taking her eyes off it. She reached a hand out, fingers inches away from the glass.

"Don't touch that!" I yelled.

"Why don't you just go away?" Rose growled.

What was wrong with her? She was acting so strange and mean. "Not until you back away from there." Didn't she remember how dangerous it was? I had to protect Rose, so I quickly stepped between her and the mirror.

Rose's eyes were fixated, staring at something past me. "Cindy?" Rose whispered. "Impossible. It can't be."

"Why are you calling for Cindy?" I asked, feeling confused.

"Scarlet?" Rose squinted, like she was trying to see something.

I grabbed Rose's shoulder and shook her. "What are you talking about?"

Rose blinked, glanced at me, then back at the mirror. "Look behind you! There! In your mirror!"

"Very funny, Rose. Haha." I fake laughed. "But I'm not falling for it."

"No. Seriously. Look, Sarah! LOOK!" Rose's finger trembled.

I put my hands on my hips. "Fine. Funny, har-har." Slowly, I turned around and faced the mirror.

On the other side of the reflection were Cindy and Scarlet.

Chapter 42

My friends were in the Underworld. There was no doubt about it. They stood on a path with ominous looking trees behind them as a monstrous shadow loomed in the distance. I knew exactly where they were. Their lips moved as they spoke something I could not hear. The shadow grabbed my friends, dragging them away.

"No!" I screamed. "He's got them!" My worms squirmed around, thudding loudly in my ears.

Steve: Looks like we've got trouble.

"Who?" Rose asked. "Sarah, what's going on? Please tell me."

"Mr. Death." I knew he'd eventually try to come for my family, but I never suspected he'd come for my friends. Now they were in danger and I was the only one who could help them. "Rose, we have to go in there!" I kicked off my slippers and threw off my robe.

Rose's eyes went wide. "You mean, go in the mirror?" She pointed at the glass surface her jaw open in disbelief.

"What else can we do?" I knew the dangers of the mirror, of the cave it led to. Although I wouldn't go through it for myself, to remove this zombie-illness, I would for my friends.

"I don't know." Rose shook her head, her red curls bouncing. "Maybe you're okay with it, but I'm certainly not going through the mirror. Look what happened to you." She covered her mouth and stepped back in horror. "I'm sorry. That's not what I meant."

Words choked in my throat and tears welled up in my eyes. How could she say such a horrible thing? I might not have looked pretty—or even human for that matter—but I was still Sarah White. Still her sister. Maybe even a better one, for that matter. The fact that she could say something so horrible and mean was like a dagger in my back. I bolted out of the room, covering my face to muffle my sobs.

"Sarah, come back!" she shouted. "I didn't mean…"

As I turned the corner I collided into Tommy, his head banging into my leg.

"Sarah not careful," he said in his high-pitched little voice.

"Sorry, Tommy." I wiped away the tears that had stained my cheeks then patted his head. "Whatcha doing little guy?"

Tommy had a strange expression on his face. "Sarah dead?" he asked around his thumb as he threaded his blanket between his fingers.

"No. I'm not dead." I was tired of him saying that.

"Sarah sick?"

I sniffled. "I guess you could say that."

"Tommy make it better." He grabbed my hand and dragged me down the stairs. When we reached the living room he pointed at the couch. "Sarah rest." He toddled off into the kitchen and I heard him rummage through the cabinet drawers.

If he only knew that his efforts wouldn't make my zombieness go away, he'd stop trying to help. Rest would never rescue my friends from the Underworld. But Tommy was too little to understand.

A minute later he returned with a hammer in his hand. "Tommy fix."

"No, no." I flinched, shielding my face. "You can't fix people with a hammer, Tommy."

"Tommy fix mirror." He smiled wide, his crooked teeth making him look a little creepy.

Creepy: Youuuuu callllllled?

"The mirror?" All the heat melted from my body and I went cold, like I'd been plunged in an icy lake.

Tommy darted up the stairs, waving the hammer.

Why would Tommy think that fixing the mirror would help me? "Wait!" I hollered. "Were you spying on us?"

But Tommy was long out of sight. And even if he could hear me, he had the uncanny knack of selective listening.

I lumbered up the stairs as fast as my zombie body could go. "Uggggghhhh," I moaned. "Tommy, answer me!" Stumbling into my room, I heard a crash. My eyes went wide, and I froze. My heart thudded. "No, Tommy. Noooo! What did you do?" I fell to the floor.

Broken glass lay scattered on the floor. Tommy held up the hammer with a thumb in his mouth. "Tommy fix."

Chapter 43

The mirror lay scattered in a million, gazillion pieces all over the floor. Tommy broke it and now there was no going back to the Underworld. Not to rescue my friends and certainly not to heal my zombie-illness.

"What am I going to do now?" I sobbed.

"What's the matter with you?" Rose asked as she returned to the bedroom. She flopped on her bed.

"Why didn't you stop him?" I growled through my teeth not even bothering to look at her.

"Stop who?" Rose asked.

I pointed at the little culprit, Tommy, and the disaster on the floor. Shattered pieces of mirror were everywhere.

Rose gasped, her hands flying up to her mouth. "Oh no! What did you do?"

"Tommy fix," he said holding up the hammer for Rose to examine.

"You didn't fix it, Tommy. You broke it." Rose ripped the hammer from his hands. "Go see Mommy."

Tommy puckered up and started to wail.

I knelt beside him feeling guilty for the way Rose and I treated him. Rose looked at me, sighed, and knelt down, too.

"I'm sorry, Tommy. We didn't mean to upset you." I snuggled him in my lap. "But you upset us when you broke this very important mirror." There wasn't time for long explanations with a three-year-old, especially when my friends were in grave danger, but if Rose and I didn't quickly diffuse this situation I might never be able to rescue them—or myself.

"Mirror bad," Tommy said between wails.

Rose made a face at me that said, *he-seems-to-know-more-than-we-do-and-he's-only-three.*

"That might be true, Tommy. But I needed the mirror so I could help my friends." I wiped his nose with a tissue. "But now I can't help them and they're in danger."

"You know what danger is right, Tommy?" Rose ruffled his hair.

"Danger is bad. Tommy doesn't want Sarah in danger."

Creepy: *Dangeeeeer isssss baaaaad.*
Crawly: *You're gonna be in danger if you go back there. Heh-heh.*
Steve: *But you have to help your friends.*

"I don't want to be in danger either. But I might never see my friends again." I turned his face and looked him in the eyes. "Do you understand?"

Tommy nodded. "Sarah no leave."

I pointed at the broken shards of glass. "Well, now I

can't." I picked up a broken piece of the mirror and dropped it on the floor defeated. It shattered into smaller pieces and Tommy flinched.

Rose carefully turned a shard of the mirror between her fingers. The afternoon sunlight reflected off its surface, bouncing around the room. This reminded me of a set of flashing lights.

"I have an idea!" I leapt to my feet, tossing Tommy mid-air.

Rose caught him before he crash-landed and we had another disaster to fix. "What is it?"

"The elevator!" I kissed Tommy's cheek then grabbed Rose's hands, twirling in a circle. "I can take the elevator."

"Have you gone mad?" Rose asked. She pursed her lips and while she furrowed one brow, raised the other.

"No," I shook my head with a laugh. "It's how I got home. It'll take me to the Underworld. That's where I will find Cindy and Scarlet." I squeezed both of Rose's hands in mine. "It'll take me straight there. I'll find them and bring them back. A few hours max and I'll be home in a jiffy. Like I was never gone. You won't even have a chance to miss me."

Rose nodded. "Good plan."

Tommy put his hands on our legs stopping our conversation. "Sarah no go to Underworld."

"But I have to, Tommy." I knelt at his side. "And you need to let me."

Tommy shook his head. "No!"

Rose gave me a look. "Remember you broke Sarah's mirror. Her very special birthday present."

Tommy lowered his head. "Sorry."

"We won't tell Mom and Dad what you did." Rose ruffled his hair.

Tommy glanced up at her.

"But you have to keep *all* of this a secret. Even the part about Sarah going to the Underworld."

"Tommy no get in trouble?" He sniffled.

"Right. You won't get in trouble." Rose's promise sounded assuring. "But you can't say anything to anyone. Understand? It'll be our secret."

"Secret." Tommy held up his pinky.

"Good," Rose said as she locked fingers with him. "Now off you go. There's a lot of work to do."

"Thank you. They're my friends and I have to help them." I hugged my sister, feeling so grateful for her support.

Rose grabbed her bow and quiver full of arrows. "You mean 'we.'"

Chapter 44

"We can leave tonight." She peered off into the distance as if scheming up a plan. "We'll have them back by morning. Then everything will return to normal. We can do this." Rose grabbed my hand and squeezed it hard.

I couldn't let her go to the Underworld. What if she turned into a zombie, too? That's not a risk I was willing to take. I had to do this on my own. "It's too dangerous."

"But I don't mind—"

BRAIN FREEZE

Yucky: What is she talking about?
Stinky: Yeah. *scratches chest* She still has her mind.
Slimy: Unlike Sarah.
Stinky: Best meal I ever ate. *belches*

"Yes. Yes, you do mind." I said. "Look at me. Do you want to turn out like this?" My ghastly green skin color and matted hair was the best method of control in this situation. Even though Rose rarely cared about her appearance or what people thought of her, I knew she cared about health. No-one would ever choose to be a zombie.

"I don't care." She folded her arms and put her nose in the air.

"But I do. I don't want you to face this same fate. I wouldn't wish it on anyone." If she only knew about my body falling apart in the Underworld and how my eyeball popped out in math class, she might think differently.

"It's not your choice to make. It's mine. And you can't stop me."

She was right. I really couldn't. And if she wanted to risk becoming a zombie, then that was her choice. I could warn her all I wanted but if she chose it for herself, then how could I stop her? I cast my gaze at the floor, unwilling to look her in the eye.

Rose tipped her head. "Listen, it'll be okay. Whatever happens, we'll deal with it together. There's worse things than being a zombie."

"As long as you understand the consequences." I eyed her from behind my matted hair.

"I was thinking a pixie cut would be cute anyway. Plus, I've always looked good in green. It's my best color." Rose smirked.

I laughed. "You're sure about this?"

"Absolutely." She threw an arm around my shoulder. "Besides, you'd be lost without me."

I playfully pushed her aside. "As if!"

"Something tells me..." she paused—her demeanor becoming serious—almost as if she didn't want to finish her sentence. "Something tells me we'll be stronger in pairs. If that shadow that took Cindy and Scarlet is any sign of what we're up against, we're going to need all the help we can get."

Rose had a point. It would be awfully difficult to defeat a monster by myself. But if there were two of us, then maybe it would be possible. "I have a feeling you're right."

"Great. Then we're agreed." She went to her dresser and rifled through a drawer. "Start packing." She tossed me a black sweatshirt.

"What do we need?" I asked. "What would help us defeat a crazed monster in the Underworld? Other than a basketful of hope and good fortune?"

"Uh...I don't know. What did you wish you had when you were there?"

My home. My family. My friends. "A way out."

Rose smiled. "Well, we're going to get out. All of us." She tossed a flashlight in the bag. "What would have made your escape easier?"

I scratched my head. "Bread crumbs." They would have kept those crows occupied. Plus, it would have been a nice reward when they helped me. "A ticket." To get into the Underworld without suspicion from Bert. "Bug spray." For all those nasty bugs, especially when Mr. Death turned into a beetle. While I wasn't sure they would have made my escape any easier, they certainly would have made my trip a little less complicated.

"Really? Bread crumbs?"

"Trust me."

"Okay." She shrugged. "If you say so. But what about the ticket and bug spray?"

I raised my eyebrows and stared at her debating

whether I should really warn her about all the things she was going to experience in the Underworld. "Do you really want to know?"

"From the sounds of it, probably not." She turned toward the door. "I'll get the bug spray while you get the ticket."

Oh right. I needed to figure out the whole ticket thing. "Good idea," I called after her as she headed downstairs. Maybe I still had the stub from the movie. That could work! But I couldn't find it. As I stood there thinking, I saw Cindy's bracelet, the one with the key. Then I remembered the Underworld ticket. Yes! I grabbed it along with Grandma Millie's necklace.

Rose grunted as she stood in the doorway, her arms loaded with a haul from the garage. "Bug repellent." She tossed the can onto her bed. "And killer," she said with a devilish grin as she dropped the second bottle of spray next to the first.

"Smart thinking."

"I also grabbed a compass while I was in the garage." Rose dumped the rest of the stuff on her bed.

"That would have been useful when..." My voice trailed off as I recalled the twisted paths in the Underworld and the time I'd spent lost in the tunnel of darkness. Rose's expression combined curiosity with anticipated horror. "Uh, never mind."

"I also found one more thing that might be useful."

"Oh yeah?"

Rose pulled a bundle of rope out of her back pocket.

Tipping my head, I grinned. Rose was pretty clever. "You might be onto something."

"I figured it might be useful if we—"

"Had to capture someone," I finished.

"Or some*thing*," she added, tossing the rope onto the bed with the rest of the stash.

"Then we're all set. Except for one last thing,"

"What's that?" Rose asked.

I clasped Grandma Millie's necklace around Rose's neck. "It's a charm."

She furrowed her brow. "What do you mean?"

"It warns of danger. You should have it. That's the way Grandma would have wanted it."

"Are you sure?" Rose closed her hand around the charm, smiling.

"I'm positive. It saved my life down there." I smiled in return, grateful to see my sister happy.

"I'm sorry I gave you such a hard time about it." Rose threw an arm over my shoulder, side-hug style.

"Don't worry about it." I hugged her back.

"Were you able to get the tickets?"

"Oh, right! I have one." I held up my Underworld ticket. "But we'll need two."

Rose's eyes lit up. "You're in luck." She went to her dresser. "Will this do?" She pulled out the stub to her movie ticket.

"You still have it?" I thought my sister hated me and every moment we spent together. Why would she have saved her ticket?

"Yeah, well, you know." She tilted her head, pursing her lips. "Mom likes to keep everything for scrapbooks. Thought I'd help her out."

"Right," I said. But I said it more like, of-course-that's-why-you-saved-it when I really wanted to say it in a sure-I'd-believe-that-in-a-million-years kind of way.

"So, what are we waiting for?" Rose tucked her ticket in her pocket. Then she grabbed her bow and quiver full of arrows and slung it over her shoulder. "Let's go!"

"Not so fast," came a voice. My eyes darted from Rose to the open door where Dad stood in the hall. "Where do you think you're going?"

Chapter 45

Dad crossed his arms waiting for a response.

"I, uh, uh—" It was a good thing my stutter sounded like my new normal zombie-talk.

"What Sarah means is that we were just coming down for dinner." Rose cocked her head. "Right, Sarah?"

I nodded. "Uh huh."

"Don't take long." Dad turned to leave but stopped and peered at us over his shoulder. "You know how Mom gets when you're late. She hates a cold meal."

"No problem, Dad." I forced a smile. It was like the ones little kids usually have in photos that says they're trying too hard. "We'll be right there."

Before going down the stairs he tapped his watch.

"That was a close one." I fell back on the bed and breathed a sigh of relief.

"Too close." Rose tightened the belt on her quiver. "Now let's go before Dad comes back. I'm guessing we have about three minutes. You ready?"

"As ready as I'll ever be." My knees may have knocked a little, but we don't need to talk about that.

"Then let's put that rope to good use." She drew it from the backpack and held it in the air, her eyes wild.

I put my hands up, surrendering. "You're not going—"

"Don't be silly." Rose opened the window and tossed one end of the rope out, while holding the other tight in her hand. "We gotta get out somehow and it can't be through the front door."

"Right." This time it was a how-could-I-have-been-so-stupid right, as opposed to the splendid-idea kind.

"You go first." Rose braced her feet against the wall. "You're lighter."

And slower. And probably not so strong since I'd become a zombie. I grabbed the rope. "Are you sure you can hold my weight?"

Slimy: I see where this is headed.
Steve: Be careful, Sarah!

"I have a twenty-two-pound draw weight on my bow. I think I can handle holding a rope with your meager eighty pounds."

"That's nearly a sixty-pound difference—"

"Just go!"

"Okay." With that, I climbed out of the window and started lowering myself to the ground. Inside, my sister grunted. "You okay?" I called.

"F..f..fine," she panted.

She didn't sound fine. In fact, I was a bit afraid she might lose her grip and drop me. I hurried down the rest of the way. "Made it!'

Rose leaned out the window. "Shhhh!"

"Sorry. Your turn," I whispered.

"All right," she said but then disappeared.

I took a step toward the house. "Rose?"

"Catch!" She tossed my backpack out the window.

My arms gave way as I caught the backpack, and the bag landed with a loud thud.

Rose shook her head. "Don't miss this one." She held up her bow and I knew she was pretty serious. If I dropped it, she'd serve my head on a platter.

"I won't," I said, catching it before it hit the ground.

"Good job," she called out the window with a smile.

"Now it's really your turn," I called up to her.

Rose took a deep breath. "Yeah, I know."

Something was bothering her. "What's wrong?"

"Uhhh....nothing." She stuck her head out the window. "I'm fine. You just…" She waved her hand at me and then started pacing. "Back up. Okay?"

"Why?" As soon as I stepped away, it dawned on me. "Who's going to hold the rope for you?"

"The lamp," she said as she hoisted herself over the window frame.

"It'll never hold you," I said, my eyes feeling like they would pop out of my skull.

Creepy: Rossssse isn't very sssssssmart, is ssssssshe?
Steve: Shhh! Let them work it out.

Crawly: But that lamp won't hold. Heh-heh. And when it doesn't. *scccretch* They're dead!
Stinky: And the whole house will know. *rubs belly* Then we can eat.
Slimy: Maybe she'll turn into a zombie, too. Then we can send our cousins over.
Icky: *sneezes* They've been looking for a new home.

"Stop it!" I said, rubbing my head.

Rose clung to the windowsill. "What's the matter?" She inched her way down the rope not waiting for my response.

"Oh, er...nothing. Just hurry." I threaded my arms through the straps of the backpack. Adjusting the bag, I noticed the lamp creeping up onto the window. "Rose! Look out!"

My sister glanced up and the lamp wobbled to and fro on the windowsill.

"Shoot!" Rose scrambled down the rope.

"It's not going to hold!" I couldn't keep my voice quiet. "Watch out!"

The lamp tumbled out of the window and Rose free-fell to the ground.

Chapter 46

A burst of air escaped Rose's lungs as she landed with a thud.

"ROSE!" I dove to her, my knees striking against the ground. We hadn't even made it to the Underworld and she'd already been hurt. If she turned into a zombie—or worse, died—I'd never forgive myself. "Rose, Rose. Wake up." I placed my hand on her cheek.

"Uhnnnn..." She moaned and blinked her eyes. "That was further than I thought."

"You mean you planned that?"

She nodded, still rubbing her head.

My sister sacrificed herself so I wouldn't have to. The sister I fought with on a daily basis (heck, sometimes it was hourly!) was willing to take one for the team. If she could do that, I really didn't know her as well as I thought, and certainly hadn't given her enough credit all these years. Instead I'd judged her on her appearance and odd behaviors, when I really should have been judging her character. The character I never bothered to know because I was too busy being worried about more trivial things. Like my own appearance. "Do you think you'll be okay?"

"It's good. I'm good." Rose wobbled to her feet. "Let's not waste any more time." She slung her bow cross-wise on her chest. Then she checked her quiver. "No broken arrows. Let's go."

We hoofed it to our destination without another word. Mostly because I wasn't sure if the elevator was there or not and if it wasn't, I didn't know exactly how to retrieve it. Probably wasn't the best time to tell her I hadn't thought it through very well.

"The cemetery?" Rose gripped her bow string.

"Uh huh." I fidgeted with the gate, but the lock was bolted tight. "What are we going to do now?"

"Give me your backpack. I've got just the thing." She rifled around in the bag and pulled out wire cutters. "This will do the trick."

"I never saw you pack those," I said, watching Rose work on the lock.

"You miss a lot, don't you?" Rose's face turned red as she squeezed the cutters. "If you're quiet and watch every now and then, you'll learn more than if you were talking all the time." She wasn't trying to be insulting because she smiled at the end. "That's why you have two eyes, two ears and only one mouth." Rose grunted with her teeth clenched together.

BRAIN FREEZE

*Stinky: And that's why my mouth is especially big. *burps**
Yucky: Yeah, it's not just for talking.
Slimy: You got that right. It's for eating like a glutton.

"Can I help?" Together we squeezed the handles and the lock snapped off. "We did it!"

"Told you it'd be best if we worked in pairs."

My sister was right. I was glad she insisted on helping me rescue Cindy and Scarlet.

"Now what?" Rose said, as she scanned the graveyard.

"This way." I waved my hand as I headed off through the headstones. "It was right here," I said pointing at the grave.

Rose placed her equipment next to the headstone. "Wait a minute."

"What?"

"This is Mrs. Stiltskin's grave." Rose shivered.

I sat next to the headstone and leaned back against it. "Yeah, I know."

"Is this a joke? Or can you really get us to the Underworld?"

My feelings were hurt that she'd think I could joke about something like that. And to use Cindy's mom as part of it would have just been cruel. "Why would I joke about this?"

Rose stepped back. "Sorry." She shook her head. "I don't know what I was thinking."

"It's okay. I kinda don't know what I was thinking either. The mirror must be the only way in and the elevator the way out."

"What are you talking about?" said a small voice. A skeleton mouse emerged from behind the grave.

"Cheddar!" I scooped him into my palm.

"The Living. Always excited. Never containing their emotions." He twitched his tail.

I lifted him to my face so we could see eye to eye socket. "Can you help us?"

"No can do." He leapt off my hand and scurried behind the headstone.

"We need your help. Please." If he couldn't get us to the Underworld, I feared for my friends and what would happen to them. With the mirror shattered into a million pieces, there was no other way to travel to the Under-world. "We're trying to rescue Cindy and Scarlet."

Cheddar poked his head around the headstone. "They said not to let anyone use the elevator."

"They *are* down there. They must have gone to help you." Rose's eyes widened as she gasped.

"The Living." Cheddar twitched his tail. "Always thinking they're so smart."

"Look, Cheddar," I shook a stern finger at him, "if you don't help us, Cindy and Scarlet might be trapped there forever. I saw them in the mirror and a horrible creature had captured them—"

"Mr. Death?" Cheddar sounded concerned, his voice choking off at the end.

"I'm not sure. It was hard to tell. Might have been the creature in the cave." I paused thinking of a way to convince Cheddar to help us. "But he's been after me. He even called Dad's cell phone. And maybe even Cindy's."

Rose wrinkled her eyebrows. "He called Dad's—"

"Never mind that," I said.

"Oh, it's him all right." Cheddar's voice was firm.

My stomach did a flip. "What do you think, Rose?"

"I'm thinking," Rose paused, gripping her bow, "this could be pretty dangerous."

"Precisely why you shouldn't go!" Cheddar scrambled behind the headstone again and his little mouse bones trembled.

"But we have to. I can't let anything bad happen to my friends." I peered around the headstone. "You care about Cindy, too. I know you do."

Cheddar twitched his tail.

"You would be considered a hero," Rose added.

Cheddar took a few steps closer. "The living. Always so concerned about being heroic."

"I bet there are medals for heroes of that caliber," Rose bribed.

"Humpf." Cheddar folded his arms.

I stole a glance with Rose. "There will be cheese. All the cheese you could ever want."

He perked his head up. "The Living. Always thinking that bribes will work." He tapped the headstone. "And they will."

A second later the bubblegum pink elevator burst out of the ground.

Chapter 47

"You won't regret this," I said, patting him on the skull. I quickly found the key hole and opened the elevator.

"The Living. Never realizing the irony in a statement like that." Cheddar scurried on board.

Trouble was, I did. But I gulped and stepped inside the elevator anyway. Rose grabbed her bow and climbed aboard, too.

"Don't worry. This is totally safe," I said as the doors closed.

The elevator made a noise and shot bullet-fast into the ground. Rose and I flew up to the ceiling. Everything jostled around, our heads banging, and our guts feeling like they'd fly out of our mouths.

"I thought you said this was safe," Rose shouted.

"I did." How could I explain that the last time I rode it, it went as slow as a turtle?

The elevator jolted to a stop and we crashed to the floor. "Umph." My undead zombie body ached.

BRAIN FREEZE

Slimy: *rubs head* Did you feel that?
Stinky: That was the thunder from down under. Here's another one. *let's one rip*
Yucky: Must you fart all the time?
Icky: That's the first time I'm thankful to have a cold. *blows nose*
Steve: Could you all control yourselves? I think she's hurt. If she's gone for good, then you know what happens to us.
Crawly: We've got to find a new home? Heh-heh.
Creepy: I don't think I'd liiiiike thaaaaaat.
Steve: Neither would I. Let's hope she's okay.

Head throbbing, I scrambled to my feet. "You all right?"

Rose took my hand and pulled herself upright. "Yeah, I think so." Then she examined her archery equipment. "The bow is good but some of my arrows are a little worse for wear." She removed a broken arrow from her quiver and tossed it aside.

"Told you it wasn't safe. Why don't the Living ever listen?" Cheddar scurried through the open door. "Hurry up now. Haven't got all day."

"Thanks, Cheddar. We've got it from here." I patted his skull.

"But you need tickets," Cheddar said in protest.

"We've got that taken care of," Rose said as she held up her movie stub.

"But you need someone to guide your way." He stood on his back paws, nibbling on his front ones.

"We have a compass," Rose said.

"But—" Cheddar started to protest again.

"We've got it from here." Rose kissed Cheddar's skull. "You keep the elevator ready."

"Humpf. Hero shmero." Cheddar crossed his arms. "You better bring me that cheese you promised."

"We will. I promise." Problem was, I didn't really know if I could fulfil that promise. The cheese wasn't the problem. Survival was.

Rose and I made it to the booth. As we approached, my heart thudded in my chest. I'd totally forgotten how Bert had ratted me out in that newspaper article. I held my ticket tight in my hand, noticing my green skin. For the first time I was grateful to be a zombie because Bert would never recognize me!

"How maaaany?" Bert asked.

"Two," Rose said sliding her fake ticket across the counter.

"How'd youuuuu get tiiiickets?" Bert asked.

Oh shoot! How could I have been so stupid? We didn't need to bring tickets, we only needed to fool Bert into giving us some.

"V.I.P.'s," Rose said.

"Hv.a.nc.dy," Bert said accepting Rose's phony ticket. I held up mine with all of my R.D. information.

As we strolled past, I kept Rose close. We avoided the Ferris wheel, and I shuddered thinking about an eternity of manning that ride with all the strange-looking kids and creatures. Out of the corner of my eye I spied the cobble-stone path that lead to all the cottages.

"This way," I said. "It will take us straight to Mrs. Stilt-skin's house."

"You mean she's here? You've talked to her?"

"Yeah." I nodded. "And I think she can help us." But then I remembered her screams when I left the Under-world. I didn't know if she survived whatever happened to her, but maybe there were clues. I pulled Rose's arm. "Just stay close and don't stray from the path."

"But why not?" Rose white knuckled her bow.

"Just..." There was so much I didn't want to explain. She was better off not knowing about any of it. We just needed to rescue Cindy and Scarlet and get home. That was our focus. Not the strange stuff in the Underworld. "Just trust me. Eyes, ears, no mouth."

"Right," she said a little too loud as she set her sight straight ahead and stepped with purpose. "I'll trust you."

"Shhh...be quiet." But it was too late. The All-Seeing Fields were awakened. They blinked their eyes.

"Ahhhhh!!" Rose scrambled backward. "What the heck is that?"

"It's the All-Seeing Fields," I whispered. "They do Mr. Death's bidding by spying on those in the Underworld. Just pretend you're a zombie and maybe they won't notice."

"Uhhhnnnn...." Rose put her hands straight out in front of her and walked with big, stiff-legged steps.

"I think that's Frankenstein," I muttered, shaking my head.

"Oh right." She changed her gait so that one leg

dragged behind her, her shoulders slumped so low they were almost on the ground. "Uhhhhnnnn...." She moaned.

"Really, Rose? Is that what you think I look like?"

Her eyes nearly bugged out of her head. "I forgot—I mean—I don't really think of you that way."

"It's fine." I lumbered past her. "Just act normal." Was that possible for her? Or me? Neither one of us really fit into a cookie cutter mold. We would probably always be different. Maybe that wasn't such a bad thing.

"Normal," she said stepping ahead.

"Shhhh."

She hunched her shoulders making herself smaller. As if this made her quieter. "Got it."

When we came to Mrs. Stiltskin's cottage the door was wide open. "This can't be!" I gasped.

Rose's posture stood as straight as the hairs on my arm. "What's wrong?"

The door was busted off its hinges and the picture window had been smashed. "Someone broke in. And I'm guessing it was none other than Mr. Death."

Rose's gaze darted to the cottage. "This is her place?"

I nodded.

"It's really cute." She touched the doorframe.

"*Was* cute," I corrected. "And I have a feeling that what we are about to find won't be adorable in the least."

Chapter 48

With courage close at hand, I stepped over the threshold. "Mrs. Stiltskin? Are you home?"

Icky: Don't be stupid, Sarah. *achoo!*
Yucky: Yeah, if you go into that house, we're all goners.

But the vast and empty darkness didn't respond to my calls.

"I don't think she's here." Rose shined her flashlight into the living room.

I exhaled softly, letting my warm breath make a puff of smoke in the cold air. It billowed in front of my face. "I had a feeling she wouldn't be."

"Where do you think—ahhhh! Ahhh ahhh!" Rose dropped the flashlight and its beam bounced around the room until it finally flickered out. She fell to the ground swatting at her head. "Get it off! Get it off!"

I darted over to her side. "What's wrong?" Then I heard the familiar sound.

"Caw!" The bird's wings beat causing the air to stir, lifting puffs of dust to dance in our faces.

"Oh, Raven!" I patted his head through a fit of coughs. "You gave us quite the fright."

"Koww!"

"You know this crazy creature?" Rose scrambled to her feet. She found the flashlight, turned it on and shined it into Raven's eyes. He blinked. Twice.

"Yeah, he's my friend." I put my hand up for Raven to sit on my finger. He transferred gingerly and snuggled into my hand as I stroked his back.

Rose fished around in my bag and pulled out the bread crumbs. "Can I feed him?"

"Good idea," I said, nearly forgetting we'd packed them. But something seemed wrong with the crow and I wasn't sure food was the answer. "Everything okay, Raven?"

Raven pecked at the crumbs in Rose's palm. "CAW!"

"We should go," I said to Rose.

"You learned that from one 'caw'?"

"That and there's a piece of red fabric over there." I pointed to a cracked window across the room. "I think Cindy and Scarlet escaped through that window."

"Using your two eyes, I see." Rose smiled. But it suddenly faded as she pointed to a gaping hole in the wall near the window. "Only something very large is capable of that kind of damage."

I nodded in agreement. We walked through the hole in the wall straight to the backyard and across the lawn, following the only two clues we had; a piece of Scarlet's cape and the evidence that something had terrorized Mrs. Stiltskin's house. Presumably Mr. Death.

"Where do you think they went?" Rose called from about ten paces back peering at the sky overhead.

"Well not up there. That's for sure."

"Sorry…" Her gaze drifted back down. She caught up and matched my pace. Breathless, she said, "I thought I saw something."

"It was probably more crows."

"Let's hope you're right. Because it seemed much larger to me. And, I dare say, it might be watching us." Rose gripped her bow. "Do you remember where you saw Cindy and Scarlet?"

"Yes. They were in the forest." I shivered, remembering my experience there. But I thought it had been destroyed after I'd gone through it. Nothing made sense in the Underworld and this was one example. Feeling an urgency to find my friends and face my demons, I quickened my pace. That same urgency told me not to go anywhere near the cave. I knew that whatever was in it would only eat us all for a snack. But I didn't have much choice.

"You know how to get there?"

"I do." I couldn't hide the hesitation in my voice, not even behind the breathlessness of my speed walk.

"Then what's wrong?"

I didn't want to scare her, but she had to know the truth. "I think we should prepare ourselves for a fight. This isn't going to be easy."

Rose gripped her bow. "I'm ready." She had no idea of what we were about to face. Frankly, neither did I.

"Good," I said, leading her through the Underworld. We hiked it past the All-Seeing Fields, Raven flying overhead like a guide. When we reached the entrance to the Dark Forest I stopped. I couldn't believe it. The forest was wide open once again. The trees arched over the path making a tunnel. Crows perched in their branches. How could that be? How could those trees have transformed, like they hadn't collapsed on each other just days ago? It didn't make sense, but then again, did anything?

I shined my flashlight down the dark path. "Are you ready for this?"

Rose nodded. "Let's do it."

"You've got to be fast." I tightened the straps on my backpack. "And by fast I mean sprint like you're trying to win the Olympic Gold. It's not a marathon. So, don't pace yourself. It's a dash, like your life depends on it. Because it does."

It became clear to me that Rose wanted to speak, that she wanted to tell me her fears, because she stared at me wide-eyed. But all of a sudden, she white knuckled her bow, nodded, then ran.

She didn't know—or forgot—that as a zombie I wouldn't be able to keep up with her. Which was all part of my plan. She'd reach our friends and save them.

I would stay behind and be the bait.

Chapter 49

Rose flew down the path, a girl on a mission. The tree branches scratched at her arms. Vines threatened to wrap around her ankles, but she swatted them off. I saw the faint glow of her necklace light the way. Crows cawed loudly and flapped in the tree-tops, sending a shower of rocks and pebbles on Rose's head. My sister was fast though. If those crows would stop all their noise, I was sure she could make it to the end, and she'd arrive without so much as a scratch.

A vine wrapped around my ankle, and I stumbled with a loud humpf, the flashlight flying from my grasp. Leaves fell to the ground as I pried the invasive weed from my leg. The vine hissed and retreated.

"Are you all right?" Rose asked.

"Fine," I shouted to her.

Rose suddenly stopped, as if she just realized I wasn't at her side. "Oh, Sarah! Let me help!"

"No. No, no." I pulled off another vine. "I'm fine. Keep going!"

"I'll be right back." Without a second of hesitation, as if Rose realized what I had done—that I'd sacrificed myself so she could go ahead—she ran toward the cave.

"I know you will." Vines wrapped around my limbs.

Knowing it wouldn't be long before Rose was in the clear, I distracted the vines. As long as they were after me, they wouldn't want her. If it kept her safe and rescued my friends, it was worth it.

Raven cawed from the treetops and, joined by a murder of crows, swooped down and lifted me into the air.

"Koww!" They crowed in unison.

"No, no. Not now." I tried to shoo them off. My only strategic plan was to be the bait. If the crows took that away, we were doomed.

"Caw, caw!" Raven cried.

I glanced up to see Rose had made it to the cave. "Alright, then. Let's go!"

We flew overhead, just skimming the umbrella of tree-tops and caught up to Rose. The crows dropped me in the opening of the cave.

"What a way to make an entrance." Rose smirked.

"We're both about to make one." I stood tall, as if it would give me courage.

We crawled into the cave, not exactly sure what we would find. But as we entered the darkness, something became abundantly clear. Although this is where we saw Cindy and Scarlet in the mirror, they were nowhere in sight. "I must have been mistaken. They're not here. Maybe this was a trap."

"You're wrong," Rose said. "They're here. I can feel it."

"I sure hope you're right." The only thing I was sure about were the worms squirming about in my head

"Cindy, Scarlet," Rose called out, her voice a raspy whisper.

A whimper came from somewhere deep in the bowels of the cavern. "Over here!" The darkness was all consuming, and I stumbled but quickly regained my footing and pushed forward.

"Here. This ought to help." A beam of light radiated from behind as Rose shined her flashlight.

"Thanks." I pointed to my right. "Down there. I think that's where the noise is coming from."

We jogged down a branch of the tunnel I hadn't seen before. It was huge, almost as though the ceiling had no limit. Very much the opposite of the tight space I'd once crawled through. I heard the noise again. "There!"

Rose pointed her flashlight down the chamber and its beam fell on Scarlet. She had a handkerchief in her mouth and she appeared to be bound by the ankles.

"You really *are* here!" My heart jumped in my chest. I never thought I'd find my friends alive. As I went to take a step forward, Rose's light began to tremble.

"A skeleton!" Rose screamed, dropping the flashlight, it's beam dancing.

"Be still," I said to Scarlet as she squirmed. "I'm coming to help."

Rose picked up the flashlight, but her hand quivered again.

"Try to calm down." I grabbed the light from her and shined it on the figure seated next to Scarlet. "It *is* a skeleton."

"Is it dead?" Rose asked.

"Of course, it is. It's a skeleton. It's not like it could be alive." The worms began squirming in my head and I quickly realized that things aren't always as they seem.

BRAIN FREEZE

Slimy: Does that mean you're dead, Sarah?
Creepy: After alllll....you do have wormsssss living in your heaaaaaad.

I thought about Cheddar. He was a skeleton, but he wasn't exactly dead, either.

"Hmpf, mmrph," came a voice from the skeleton.

As I watched the skeleton writhe in place, a sparkly barrette grabbed my attention. The same barrette that Cindy always wore. "Wait a minute!" I took one shaky step forward. "Cindy, is that you?"

The skeleton nodded.

In my panic and disbelief, I fell to my knees, dropping the flashlight. "How is that even possible?" Thoughts buzzed around in my head, but nothing made sense. "Never mind. That doesn't matter. I'm a zombie, so there's that." I held out my green-skinned arms and then crawled toward my friends.

Cindy and Scarlet were tied together, back to back. Handkerchiefs gagged their mouths.

Rose tossed me a pocket knife.

"You thought of everything," I said to Rose, amazed at her preparation. Knife in hand, I cut through a rope. "I'll get you out. I promise." Hunter had made promises, too, but he never followed through. In fact, I hadn't seen him in so long I almost felt like I would forget him.

"Mmmffph," Scarlet mumbled with wide eyes.

Cindy shook her head.

"It's fine. We're here. Everything is going to be okay now. Right, Rose?"

But Rose stood frozen in place, as her necklace glowed and pulsed. A warning. Her breath came in shallow waves and a tear escaped her eye and rolled down her cheek.

"What's wrong?" I picked up the flashlight and shined it at her.

A giant, three-headed dog stood behind Rose, foaming at the mouth.

Chapter 50

The saliva dripped onto the ground, collecting in a pool. It splattered onto Rose's shoes. The hound growled, a low, deep guttural sound. Then it lunged at her.

Rose ducked. One of the hound's heads smashed against the cavern's wall. The beastly dog howled in pain.

"Goooo!" Rose screamed, nearly colliding into me, the flashlight slipping from my fingers. Its bright white beam dimmed to a narrow, soft yellow hue before dying out completely. When Rose and I were face-to-face, she shook my shoulders. "We have to get out of here!"

But I ignored her plea, staring, instead, at the giant monster. Brown, mangy fur spotted the dog's body in uneven clumps. Its pointed ears—all six of them—were sharp as razors. The hair on the beast's hackles stood in spikes. Giant paws, dug at the ground, ready to charge.

I turned back to Cindy and cut through another piece of rope. "Rose, you've got to help me! I can't do this alone."

Rose blinked and dashed to my side. She began untying the rope which kept the girls bound together while I sawed away at the binding on their wrists.

With one of Cindy's hands now free, she pulled the handkerchief from her mouth. "Hurry. It's coming! There's not much time." Cindy fumbled with the one free hand to help untie another rope.

Scarlet snarled through her handkerchief and wrinkled her nose.

"I'm going as fast as I can," I said to Scarlet.

"I'll get it," Rose said, trying to remain calm.

Cindy pulled her other hand free. "Don't worry. She's not directing that at you." She started untying the ropes around her ankles.

Scarlet broke free from the last rope as I cut through the final thread. She pulled the cloth from her mouth. "Get him! Get the beast!" Scarlet said. Something small flew off her shoulder and dive bombed the giant dog. "Good boy, Shade!"

"A bat!" I ducked down, afraid of it tangling in my hair.

Scarlet shook off the ropes and stood up. "Yes. Shade will help us."

The bat dove at the dog, grabbing at his fur. The beast howled, then chomped at the air.

"You three go ahead. I've got this," Scarlet said as she smiled wide, exposing a very large, very sharp set of fangs.

"Vamp….vamp…vampire!" Rose pointed a finger at Scarlet.

"Cheese and rice!" I said. "You're a vampire?"

"And you're a zombie. Your point is?" Scarlet's frank response made me blink. "Now get out of here. I've got this."

Cindy, Rose, and I scrambled out of the cave, while Scarlet remained behind.

A loud howl echoed from within the cavern and, instinctively, I covered my ears. Seconds later Scarlet burst through the mouth of the cave, landing with a thud on the ground.

"What happened?" Cindy asked.

"You don't want to know," Scarlet replied. "But you better run. I'm pretty sure he's mad as heck."

"You didn't..." Cindy started to say.

"I did." Scarlet didn't clarify, but it seemed as though they understood each other.

Nervous, I glanced back to see three pairs of red eyes glowing in the darkness. Six eyes burning like small charcoal embers. Six eyes that wanted us dead. A high-pitched howl sent a warning. But I sensed pain in that sound, too. Whatever Scarlet had done, it didn't go over too well. Strange because I never saw her as the violent type.

Rose craned her neck to look back at the cave.

"Do you think—" I started to say.

"RUN!" Rose said, her eyes as big as dinner plates. "RUNNNNN!"

As I kicked it into high gear, I remembered that my zombie body didn't really have a high gear. It had one gear. Slow.

Warm air breathed down on me and the hairs on the back of my neck stood on end. A tree root squirmed its way out of the ground and I stumbled. Sharp pain shot up my leg as it snapped. Then I tumbled to the ground. My chin smacked against a rock, teeth clanging together. When I looked up, Rose stood straight and stiff with her bow drawn.

"I can't move," I said. "I think it's broken." The pain in

my leg was immense and I didn't see any way that I could get out of this situation. "Please don't miss, Rose, or this is the last you'll see of me." There was no question that beast would eat me as a snack.

"Don't hurt him," Cindy pleaded. Her voice sounded concerned but because she was a skeleton it was impossible to read the expression on her face.

"Kill it." Scarlet's voice, on the other hand, contained fierce determination. Shade sat on her shoulder and she patted him. "Go for the jugular."

"The shoulder," Cindy whispered. "Please. Just the shoulder." Her voice choked on each word.

Rose prepared to release, squinting as she aimed. *Just get rid of the monster*, I thought as it towered over me. I didn't say it out loud because I didn't want to hurt Cindy's feelings. She seemed truly concerned that no one should harm this three-headed hound. As my green skin contrasted against the Dark Forest, I realized that I was, in fact, a monster, too. And so were both of my friends. Who was I to judge another? Still, it was my life or the beast. I'd choose my own.

Rose's arm trembled as she held her position, ready to fire. Cindy flinched and turned away.

The three-headed hound drooled on my leg, his hot breath right over me.

If Rose didn't release soon, there really would be a dead thing.

Me.

 BRAIN FREEZE

Slimy: Dead things. I like dead things.
*Stinky: Best place to eat. *Burps**
Creepy: And liiiiiiive.
Steve: Sarah's not dead.
*Icky: Not yet. *Achoo!**
Steve: Let's not be responsible for her demise, either.

I rubbed my head. Stupid worms. "Hurry," I said, my voice tight in my chest, every part of my body aching. "What are you waiting for? Do it!"

Rose's eyes narrowed as she aimed directly at the beast's jugular. The bow twanged and the arrow soared through the air.

Chapter 51

The arrow grazed the hound's shoulder and the dog barked, almost like it was laughing at Rose's bad aim. He shook his body and wads of drool flung out everywhere, along with a few stray pieces of fur.

"You missed," Scarlet said. Her brow furrowed, as if in disgust. "How could you miss?"

Cindy lowered her hands. "She did?" Her eyes brightened as she glanced at Rose before whipping her head toward the hound. "It'll be okay," she said with a sigh. But the hound didn't seem to care about Cindy's promise because it only barked louder.

Rose and Scarlet helped me to my feet. The hound lunged and then yipped. A long, metal chain around its neck clanged and yanked the dog backward

"He's tied?" I asked.

"Looks that way," Scarlet said. "Anchored to the inside of the cave."

"But that chain could break any minute, so we better get out of here." Rose slung her bow over her shoulder.

Cindy and Scarlet lent me their shoulders, and we lumbered forward, my leg bent at an odd angle. A large tear in my jeans revealed blood running down my leg. It exposed something else. My bone. Specifically, my fibula.

Feeling suddenly dizzy, I fell to the ground and my vision went dark.

"Sarah," Cindy's sweet voice called. "Sarah, wake up."

My eyelids fluttered and I moaned.

"Oh, get up!" Rose said as a stinging sensation burned my cheek.

My eyelids burst wide open.

"You slapped her?" Scarlet looked at Rose, her mouth frozen in an 'O.'

"I had to," Rose said. "Besides, she understands. Don't you, Sarah?"

I rubbed my head. "I do?" Where was I anyway? What was happening? And why did my leg throb? Shifting, I saw the bone sticking out and remembered everything. My head wobbled and my vision went fuzzy.

BRAIN FREEZE

Slimy: See! She's gonna die!
Stinky: *Rubs belly* Then we can eat.
Steve: She's not going to die. And stop talking about food. You just ate.

"Oh no you're not," Cindy said, grabbing my face in her hands. "You're not passing out again. Stand up on your one good leg and walk, do you hear me? We're going to get out of here. Together." Her eyes pierced mine and I felt her determination.

"Okay." Nodding, I reached out to her. "Help me up."

Cindy and Scarlet brought me to my feet, and I used their shoulders for support again.

The hound howled and growled and then lunged forward, snapping his jaws. We might have been temporarily out of reach, but we definitely weren't safe for long.

The hound lunged forward a second time. Then a third.

"It's not going to hold." Scarlet pointed at a loose link in the dog's chain. With each lunge, the link bent, opening at the seam.

"Smart dog," Rose said.

Shade shifted from Scarlet's hair down to her shoulder. "Dogs are never smart. They're nasty, smelly, drooling blobs of fur." Scarlet's boots pounded against the trail making a steady beat.

"And that drooling blob of fur," Rose threw a thumb over her shoulder, "wants to eat you for lunch."

"He already knows I'd make a terrible snack." Scarlet's voice rang in my ears as she shifted under the weight of my arms. She grunted, still trying to carry me. "I'm much too sour."

I stifled a snicker, then flinched through the pain throbbing in my broken leg. A sound burst through my lips, a combination of a laugh coupled with a cry of pain.

And just as it did, another sound struck me. A giant cracking snap and the clang of the hound's metal chain clattering to the ground.

Chapter 52

Cindy glanced back over her shoulder. "He broke it!" Her eyes bulged out of her skull. "Run, run, run!"

But I couldn't. Not as a zombie and certainly not with a broken leg. "Go without me," I said, breaking free from Cindy and Scarlet's supportive shoulders.

"No way. I'm not leaving you behind." Cindy's eyes met mine.

"It's okay. This was the plan all along. I came to save you and Scarlet." What I didn't tell her was that I never committed to saving myself

Creepy: Luuuuunch.
Stinky: It's about time.
Steve: Sarah, I know you have a plan that doesn't include self-sacrifice. Think fast!

"I won't let you do this." Cindy reached out for a hug.

"Just go before I change my mind." I shoved her away, my fingers slipping between her boney ribs.

Scarlet grabbed Cindy's skeleton hand. "We've escaped worse things together. We can manage this one, too."

"Koww!" The friendly sound of Raven's cawing brought a smile to my face in an otherwise dark moment. He circled twice before going in for the landing. He dove down striking my shoulder. Raven's claws dug in deep. I patted his head, feeling grateful that I wouldn't have to endure this alone.

Scarlet set her face. "I'll be back for you."

"I know you will." Even if she did mean it, there wouldn't be enough time. "It's okay. I have an idea," I said, drawing the breadcrumbs from the pocket of my bag. I tipped my head toward the crows.

"Brilliant!" Scarlet nodded. "It might just work." She patted Shade's head. "Send for help, okay boy?" Shade flew off into the darkness of the forest without hesitation.

Suddenly, the hound growled. He was gaining on us, his sharp teeth closer than I dared imagine. I'd be a double dead girl by the time Scarlet returned. "I've got this. Now go!"

"Koww," cried Raven. "Koww."

Rose, Scarlet, and Cindy took off, running like I'd never seen them run before.

They were only halfway through the Dark Forest when a thunderous noise shook the ground. My friends toppled like dominos.

In the distance behind me, near the mouth of the cave, a giant shadow with large claws and a massive rounded body took one steady step after another, the ground quaking with each one.

A stifled scream burned my throat and acid crept into my mouth. I scrambled to my feet and lumbered forward.

The three-headed hound made incredible gains. I glanced up at the treetops. A very large murder of crows had gathered, watching the demise unfold. I needed to time it just right or my plan wouldn't work.

The hound's paws pounded on the ground; the bird's beady eyes watched.

"Who'd like a snack?" I said, taking out a handful of crumbs. I threw them at the dog and the murder of crows flew like bullets. I tossed another handful, this one landing on the hound's head. The birds pecked and pecked while cawing loudly over their meal. The beast collapsed on the ground, howling in pain.

With the dog incapacitated, I hobbled forward to catch up to my friends who were sprinting toward the clearing. Soon they would be in the All-Seeing Fields, free from the dangers of the Dark Forest, but subject to the spying eyes of Mr. Death.

If I didn't move faster, I would be a sitting duck. I pressed through the pain, willing it to go away and forcing my legs to run. Whatever that shadow creature was, it would certainly take what remained of my zombie-life. I knew this because it was the same shadow, I'd seen tormenting Cindy and Scarlet in the mirror.

Which made me think about something. I saw Cindy, not a skeleton, in the mirror. Did the shadow or even Mr. Death do this to her? Or was the mirror just a rouse to get me back to the Underworld? I might never really know the answers to these questions because I would probably never make it out of here. This creature would kill me first.

Another step thundered from the shadow and a sharp cry from the hound soon followed. Turning, I saw the beast tuck his tail. He whimpered and cried. The crows flew back to the treetops. Then the hound howled and yelped, cowering when a snap rang out.

Mr. Death stood, five times his normal size, whipping the dog into submission with a giant boney vine. But Mr. Death looked different. He had antenna like a beetle and two additional arms. My heart thudded wildly. Limping forward the All-Seeing Fields were just a few steps away. "Almost there," I said with a grunt. A hand grabbed the neck of my shirt and pulled me back into the forest. "Noooo!" I cried. Raven flew off, cawing loudly. My friends stopped in their tracks and turned around. Their jaws came unhinged when they saw me dangling mid-air.

Chapter 53

"Sarah!" Cindy screamed.

"Just go!" My heart thudded and tears threatened to escape my eyes. There was nothing they could do to save me. They needed to escape, no matter what.

"Where do you think you're going?" boomed the voice holding me captive.

"Mr. Death!" Cindy gasped.

Why didn't I realize it was him all along? It was always Mr. Death in all his various shapes and forms. He was the one in charge. And he also seemed to have some sort of vendetta. Why else would we all be gathered here at the same time?

"You don't scare us," Scarlet said, her voice firm but I could hear the quiver revealing her fear. She flung her torn red cape over her shoulder and exposed her fangs. "Now let her go!"

"Never!" Mr. Death laughed, his back to the Dark Forest. "Now it's time for supper!"

He raised me to his giant mouth. It opened like a calla lily, his lips curling outward, his tongue a stamen with a bulbous tip. His breath smelled of rotting flesh. Mr. Death was nothing more than a living corpse.

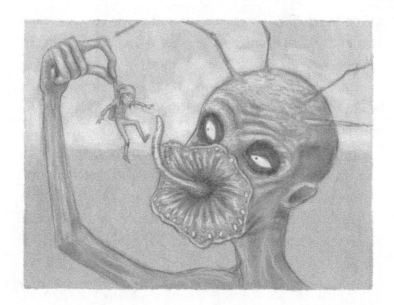

I covered my eyes and held my breath.

"Put her down!" Scarlet kicked his enormous ankle.

"Now why would I do that? I have her right where I need her." Mr. Death rang my body like a bell, jingling me about in the air. "If I'm to become human again—and finally live—then I need every first-born child I can get. Young life will give me eternal life."

Cindy picked up a rock and threw it at him. "You'll never be alive!"

"Besides," Rose folded her arms with an air of confidence despite her necklace strobing a warning. "These girls are all dead." She pointed at me. "You're about to eat a zombie. And that one?" She pointed at Cindy. "She's a skeleton. Can't imagine there's much life left there."

Cindy turned her head sharply. "Hey, watch it!"

Rose narrowed her eyes and nodded, as if she were

trying to tell Cindy to relax. Rose then waved her hand at Scarlet. "And that one's a vampire. Who knows how long she's been dead."

Mr. Death seemed to consider this for a moment, his beady, gem-like black eyes darting from me to each of my friends.

"If it's a first born you need, then you're going to want me. I'm the oldest. Not Sarah." Technically, we were both firstborns, since we were half-sisters. Same mother, different fathers. But Rose straightened and I saw her fingers slide across her bowstring. My genius sister had an incredible idea. If I had anything to say about it, I was going to help her pull it off! "So if it's life you're after, you'll have to take mine."

"NOOOOO!" I screamed, playing along with her mind game. Even if it didn't work, I was already dead. Who cared if he took me? But if her plan was a success, then we'd all be free, and Mr. Death would be gone for good. At least I hoped.

Mr. Death's tongue slithered out of his mouth, the tip of it licking the air around me, breathing and sensing like a snake.

"You don't want either of them. I'm not dead and you know it as well as I do." Cindy climbed up Mr. Death's leg. "You know I'm a first born."

"No, Cindy, don't!" I tried to give her a look, but her eyes darted from Mr. Death to me. She was playing along, too. I had some really smart friends.

"Mr. Death! I know who you are! You're Riddick Stilt-skin!" a voice shouted from the All-Seeing Fields. It was Cindy's mom, Mrs. Stiltskin.

"Great-grandpa Stiltskin?" Cindy gasped and lost her footing. She tumbled halfway down before grasping onto his pant leg.

"Not quite. I'm his twin brother. Your great-grand-uncle," Mr. Death said with a laugh.

"He had a brother? I never knew." Mrs. Stiltskin gasped. Then her eyes grew wide. "Wait a minute. I've heard stories about you! You were jealous of your brother. His wife had spun straw into gold and you wanted it all to yourself. You're Rumple Stiltskin! "

"The one and only!" Mr. Death bowed. "And now I'm going to claim the promise made to me over a century ago; the first born of each family. Then I can be human again and live to see another day."

"No, you won't." Mrs. Stiltskin marched forward. "You'll never take these children or any others ever again!" She stood at the entrance of the Dark Forest her hands clenched in tight fists. "Over my dead body."

"Well, if you insist!" Mr. Death—Rumple Stiltskin—sent a vine shooting from his waist. It wrapped itself around Mrs. Stiltskin's body. Another vine covered her mouth. Mr. Death shook the vines and Mrs. Stiltskin jerked into the air like a yo-yo. Without warning, he flung her hard. Muffled cries floated into the air as her body whipped into the forest, crashing against a wall of trees. Her body snapped and she lay lifeless on the path within the Dark Forest.

"Mom! Mom!" Cindy jumped from Rumple's leg and dashed toward her mother. "Mom are you okay? Please tell me you're all right!" she screamed with each stride. When she reached her mother, she knelt at her side.

Cindy threw her arms around Mrs. Stiltskin who was unresponsive. Cindy sobbed, her shoulders shaking violently. After a moment, she wiped her eyes and turned to Mr. Death. "You're nothing but a monster! You killed my mother!" Cindy's voice changed and I was afraid my friend might never be the same again. Her eyes lit like flames from a fire. "You're going to pay for this."

"She was already dead," Rumple reminded her with a laugh.

"My mom was a first born." Cindy's bones clattered as she inched toward her great-grand uncle. "You took her from me the first time, too, didn't you?"

"You know me well, don't you dear?" Rumple threw his head back and laughed. "Now, time for lunch." He flicked me from his hand, and I sailed into the forest. Then he grabbed my sister.

Chapter 54

My arms flailed as I tried to grab anything within reach. If I slammed into the ground, I had a feeling I'd suffer a similar fate as Cindy's mom. Desperate, I reached for a tree branch, but it slipped from my fingers. Then I landed on something incredibly soft, bouncing twice before hitting the ground. As I scrambled to my feet, I saw that the three-headed dog had been my landing pad. Half expecting the monster to attack me, I stumbled away but the dog didn't move. He was covered in lacerations which looked severe.

Rose dangled in the air, precariously close to Rumple's mouth. "Get the rope! And the spray!" she yelled. "Hurry!"

"Toss it here," Cindy said.

I threw the rope to her, but she gave it to Scarlet instead. As Rumple was distracted, ready to eat my sister as a snack, I stuffed the bug spray in my pocket, then fought the pain and hobbled closer. A make-shift bandage might buy me some relief, so I ripped my pant leg off and tied it around my broken leg. Once it was secured, I scrambled up Rumple's giant body straight up to his enormous head.

"It's supper time!" Rumple said as he drooled.

"Not if I have anything to say about it!" I sprayed the bug repellent into his eyes.

Rumple roared. "You really think that will work on me?" He wiped away the chemicals then laughed. "You little gnat. Stop being a pest." He swatted me and I tumbled down, catching onto the belt loop of his pants.

"No, but this will." Rose raised her bow.

"What's that?" Rumple asked, squinting.

"He can't see!" I yelled. "The spray has blinded him!"

"Can't do it," Rose said, squirming in Rumple's grip. "Need more room."

"Just try! I believe in you!" I shouted up to my sister.

Rose nodded, pursed her lips, and nocked her arrow. She took a breath then drew back, holding steady as she aimed.

Rumple blinked as he dangled Rose from his fingers. "Time to die!"

"You bet it is." Rose released the string. The arrow soared through the air. It lodged between Mr. Death's eyes.

Rumple roared and swayed. His eyes rolled back in his head.

"Bullseye," Rose said, lowering her bow with a satisfied grin.

At the same time, Scarlet lassoed the rope, whipping around Rumple's ankles. She tugged, and he fell backward with a tremendous crash. Rose and I toppled to the ground and wiggled free from Death's grasp.

My sister ran toward me and I embraced her. "You did it. I knew you could."

The three-headed hound began howling. He raised his

hackles and writhed painfully on the ground. Cindy sprinted to the creature.

"Don't..." I started to say but stopped. Cindy must know what she was doing.

The hound thrashed and then split into three individual dogs. They threw their heads back and howled in unison.

"It's okay," Cindy tried to comfort the beasts, which now resembled a trembling pile of bloody crow-pecked wolves.

Werewolves to be exact.

Each wolf shook, sending bits and pieces of fur flying through the air. That once three-headed hound was now three boys.

"Hunter? Is that really you?" Limping over to him, I felt my heart beating so fast I thought it might burst.

Nursing his wounds, Hunter met me halfway. "I told you I'd find you." He hugged me tight.

"But that day in the mirror...you were so angry. So fierce."

"Of course, I was angry. I knew you'd been taken by Mr. Death." He puffed loudly, lifting up the hem of his shirt, revealing a large gash. "I told you to run because I was going to jump through the mirror after you. Didn't want to hit you on the way in."

"You risked your life?" My eyes leaked tears of joy. "You really kept your promise. Even if you did try to kill me in the process." I laughed.

"Sorry about that." Hunter wrapped his arm around my shoulder and pointed at the two other boys. Ethan, who I knew, but another that I didn't recognize. "This is my brother, Maurice."

Maurice licked his hand which still had a patch of dog fur on it. "Thank you for helping us. And sorry for giving you all a scare."

"Mr. Death, I mean Rumple Stiltskin, had us under his spell, completely at his will and command," Ethan said as he scratched behind his ear. A couple of fleas fell onto the ground. He turned and hugged his new-found brother. "Mom and Dad are going to be so happy. They're never going to believe where you've been all this time."

"I had no idea you had another brother," I said, resting my head against Hunter's shoulder.

"He's been missing since infancy. First born." Hunter patted Maurice's back. "But Mr. Death couldn't use his soul because of the werewolf blood."

"That's why I didn't want Rose to harm them," Cindy admitted as she threw her arms around Ethan in a hug.

I nodded, understanding everything. "Let's get out of here."

A growl rumbled from deep in the Dark Forest and vines shot out from the darkness. We all froze.

Tree branches shook and the murder of crows swooped down. Their wings beat furiously as they pecked at Rumple's body. Raven jabbed out Rumple's eyes, which sparkled like two onyx gemstones. The bird dropped the stones into my hand. An unsettling feeling washed over me as I slipped them in my pocket.

Shade returned with a colony of bats. They swarmed around Rumple's body tearing at his flesh as if it were made of millions of small bugs. The trees wrapped their branches around Rumple Stiltskin's upper limbs.

"He's dead," I sighed with relief.

Rose pointed to her necklace, which was still glowing. "I don't think so."

Mr. Stiltskin's legs fired to life and flailed as a garbled warning boomed from his mouth. "This isn't the end."

Chapter 55

T he trees sucked Rumple in like a thirsty child with a slurpee and he disappeared into the Dark Forest. Rose's necklace pulsed a bright white light then went dark.

Mrs. Stiltskin floated out of the Dark Forest, her skin glowing. Cheddar sat in the palm of her hand. "It's over." She smiled softly. "I made sure the forest took care of him."

"Thank you." Cindy's eyes flooded with tears, seeing her mom again, this time as a beautiful angel.

"Goodbye, my darling girl," Mrs. Stiltskin said as she smoothed Cindy's cheek.

Cindy returned the touch as tears soaked her face. "I love you, Mom."

"The Living. Always with the mushy sentiments," Cheddar harrumphed as he crossed his arms. "I never did get that cheese."

"You're my hero. You're stronger than I could ever dream to be." Mrs. Stiltskin kissed the top of Cindy's head. "You'll always be my girl. I will love you forever and all eternity." Mrs. Stiltskin tapped Cindy's chest and then gasped one last breath. Her body shimmered and glittered, twinkling like stars in the sky. It began to fade until Mrs.

Stiltskin became translucent. Then, both she and Cheddar disappeared.

"No!" Cindy cried. "Mom, don't go!" She fell to the ground and sobbed.

We swarmed around Cindy, embracing her. Her body shook so hard from the sobs, I could feel it deep in my core.

"I'm sorry," I said. There were never good words at a time like this. Everything felt so inferior. I squeezed her tighter. "She'll always be with you. Somehow. Somewhere." I'd never lost someone I loved and had no idea how much she hurt, but giving her comfort seemed the only reasonable thing.

Cindy continued to cry, and we all stood wordlessly, embracing her with a friendship that would unite us forever. Rose's necklace began to sparkle with a pink hue. Something had changed. We all stepped back and peered up, watching the bats soaring in the sky, shimmering like dark stars.

Shade flew onto Scarlet's shoulder and nestled against her chin. She patted his head. "You're a good bat, Shade."

An abrupt gust of wind brought our attention skyward again. The crows cawed and flapped their wings furiously. Raven joined them. My heart ached with sadness as I watched him fly away.

The crows changed shape, their feathers bursting off and showering down on us. I flinched, shielding my face expecting stones. But, to my amazement, I didn't feel rocks. I peeked between my forearms and saw the sky littered with beautiful, inky black feathers. They floated softly to the ground.

The dark feathers were replaced with white ones and the former crows were now doves. They changed shape again, morphing from birds to humans. It was suddenly clear the crows had become angels. They floated in the sky, with downy white wings, and halos circling their heads in crowns of glorious gold.

"Angels." Cindy pointed at the sky.

"Guardian angels," I said, knowing that's what they really were. Those crows had tried to save me. Only guardian angels would be helpers like that.

Mid-flight, Raven morphed into an angel. He hovered just above the ground. Raven stretched out a hand and I stepped closer. When our faces were nearly touching, he kissed my cheek. A tingling sensation rippled over my skin. "Thank you," Raven said. His voice sounded like music, the soft bowing of a violin. A stark contrast to his former cawing. He glowed so brightly I couldn't see his features, yet I knew he was smiling in that light.

"No." I shook my head. "Thank *you*." Raven had saved me. Had helped me when I was lost. Had led me to safety and protection. Helped me find myself when I didn't know who I was.

Raven's silhouette shimmered and then he spread his wings. They flapped hard creating a gust of wind.

My hair blew into my face as I watched the Dark Forest close in. The branches of the trees reached across and linked together until the path was entirely sealed. The garbled mess of branches and vines, twigs and roots solidified into a solid wall of rock.

Goosebumps rose up on my arms as a whoosh of cool air came from behind. The eyes in the All-Seeing Fields rose up into misty figures. "We're free," the ghosts of children whispered in unison. "Thank you." They floated into the heavens, each taking one of the angels' hands and disappearing into the light.

Raven flapped his beautiful wings. "Goodbye Sarah," he said, before darting into the open sky, flying free for what I could only assume was a very long time. As he soared to freedom, I missed him already. And yet, somehow, I knew he'd always be there to guide me.

"He's gone," Scarlet said.

"I know. They all are." It was for the best. Raven, the crows, and the children were free. So were Mrs. Stiltskin and Cheddar. Rumple was in outer darkness, exactly where he belonged.

"You did it." Cindy wrapped her arms around Rose.

I wiped away a tear that had formed in the corner of my eye. "You really did." I put my hand on Rose's shoulder. But she shrugged my hand off. Then, with a smile, she threw her arms around my neck and hugged me tight.

The boys howled in excitement then laughed at themselves.

"*We* did it," Rose said. "All of us. Together."

And we had.

EPILOGUE

I swept up the pieces of broken mirror and dumped them in the trash. Enough of that nonsense. Our family was going to be safe. No more magical mirror portals. No more danger. A two-inch-wide, three-inch-long shard shaped like Florida reflected the light from my dresser and instinctively, I reached in and grabbed it. "You've caused an awful lot of trouble," I said to the broken shard of mirror. Actually, it was Mr. Death —Rumple Stiltskin—who had been the troublemaker. The mirror was just part of it. I rubbed my head, missing the chatter from the noisy, disgusting little worms. They must have dried up when everything ended in the Underworld.

Rose walked in and smiled. "Feeling better?" she asked.

"Yeah," I ran my fingers through my hair.

"Glad to see you're back to your normal color." Rose hugged me.

There were a few scars but other than that, my lovely sun-kissed tan had returned. "You and me both."

"I'm going to make lunch. Want anything?"

"No thanks." A group text lit up my phone. Distracted, I placed the shard of glass on my dresser. Cindy, Scarlet, Ethan, Hunter, Maurice, Rose, and I all exchanged funny emojis. Then, a moment later, I grabbed the trash can and hobbled down the stairs, my cast thumping the whole way. With extreme pleasure, I emptied the mirror remnants into a bag, tied it all up, and brought it to the curb for the trash men. "Wait," I said, gimping after them. "One last bag."

The truck stopped and a man hopped off the back. He took the trash and threw it into the compactor. Satisfied, I watched them drive off then returned to the house.

Relieved, I climbed the stairs two at a time. When I reached my room, I stood in the doorway, wondering why my mom was there.

My mom had her back turned. She lifted the shard of mirror, fluffed her hair, and gazed deeply into it. "Mirror, mirror..."

ACKNOWLEDGMENTS

Special thanks to all the zombies who made this book possible. No, I would never be talking about my dearest sisters in the morning.

Thanks to my bike whose long rides kept my thoughts rolling. "They see me rollin', they hatin'."

— BETHANIE BORST

Many thanks to my friends, crit partners, beta readers, and the author community. A special thanks to Tim, who I can always count on, even in a pinch.

Thanks to my family for their constant support and never-ending supply of chocolate. And love. Definitely huge thanks for that.

To my readers, thank you for sticking with me through this series. Many obstacles, which were out of my control, delayed this book for far too long. Thank you so much for your patience. Your enthusiasm is contagious and every bit of fan mail has lifted me up.

May you have many Scarily Ever Laughters in your future!

— AMIE BORST

ABOUT THE AUTHOR

Amie Borst loves glitter, unicorns, and chocolate. But not glitter covered chocolate unicorns. That would be weird. She's a PAL member of the SCBWI as well as a founding member of *The Mixed-Up Files of Middle-Grade Authors*, a group blog dedicated to middle-grade books. She's also a judge on *Rate Your Story*. While she'd like to travel the world in a hot pink elevator, she's content to write more books from the comfort of her home in Virginia.

For updates and a free ebook, visit her website.
www.amieborst.com

f facebook.com/amieborstauthor

instagram.com/amieborst

ABOUT THE CO-AUTHOR

Bethanie Borst is the 19 year old mastermind and co-author of the Scarily Ever Laughter series. She was only 10 when she wrote Cinderskella, 12 when she signed her first book deal, and 13 when it went to publication. At 15 she wrote Snow Fright and upon its launch, was 16. Now, at the rerelease and second edition, she's 19 and a college student. She enjoys reading, writing, and STEM. Bethanie is fluent in both sarcasm and humor and is prepared for the zombie apocalypse and/or spontaneous combustion of the world. Because, let's face it, both of those things are totally legit. Learn more about Bethanie at her website. www.amieandbethanieborst.com

[f] facebook.com/amieandbethanieborst

ABOUT THE ILLUSTRATOR

Roch Hercka is an illustrator, painter, and book lover. He has been drawing for as long as he can remember. Inspiration for his work comes from dreams (mostly the bad ones), spooky folk stories, and music. Roch has always been attracted to all things dark, scary, and grim, while also having a fascination of the beautiful world around him. Roch is a fan of comic books, board games, movies, and food. He lives and works in Torun, Poland with his family and a cat.

Illustrations: www.hercka.carbonmade.com
Paintings: www.roch.carbonmade.com

facebook.com/Hercka.art
instagram.com/rochart_85

ALSO BY AMIE BORST

Doomy Prepper series:

Doomy Prepper's Complete Guide: How To Survive Fifth Grade and the Apocalypse

Unicorn Tales series:

Callie's Magical Flight

Maeve's New Friend

Elle's Secret Wish

Nadia's True Colors

Maribel's Windy Rescue

Fiona's Missing Shell

Bonnie's Enchanted Blossoms

Morgan's Harvest Festival

Free ebook:

Dead Chimes

CPSIA information can be obtained
at www.ICGtesting.com
Printed in the USA
LVHW051636021120
670484LV00002B/245